BEND THE BLUE SKY

A NOVEL

Conversations with Crows Press
P.O. Box 2763
Avon, Colorado 81620
www.cwcpress.com

BEND THE BLUE SKY

ISBN Number: 978-1-63173-537-0

Printed in the United States of America

. . . for my father, who changed things as they were

Acknowledgments

Dwaine, my beloved, for knowing what is art and what is real and for loving both.

Rakai and Taiaroa...how much I want to be worthy of your perfect love.

My mother for showing me how to be the wife of a great man and for loving me up in the best way.

The midwives of this work:
Kerry Balaam, Betsy Boland, Marisa Powers, Meghann Schroers-Martin, Morgan Taylor, Basia Wasowski, Andrea Weimer and Debbi Wraga.

Pat Schneider for reminding me of Emily Dickinson's fascicles, for guiding me into my independence, for being the model I needed…exactly when I needed one.

Virginia Woolf for the image of "letting the atoms fall as they may"…and for the infinite inspiration of her life and work.

Patti Page for reminding me of something I never knew but have always loved.

Susan Teare and Nicholas Bell for the gift of your art and friendship.

Kristina Rockhold Perino for everything that you were to me in those desperate days…and for continuing to be such a dear friend.

In Gratitude…

Ever.

BEND THE BLUE SKY

A NOVEL

Kim Cope Tait

Conversations with Crows Press

Avon

2015

Chapter One

September 1952, Bradford, Arkansas

Violet was on the porch sweeping. The sun lumbered behind the elms that lined the railroad track at the end of the road. She had the baby on her hip, and my father Matthew (he is nearly three in this memory and still goes by Matty) was bulldozing the defunct garden with his toy truck. It was starkly yellow against the brown earth, pale in its aridity, even after it had been churned like this by tiny wheels and hands. The air was barely moving, and Violet could hear the low hum of a radio far off. Across the way in the neighbor's sage-colored house maybe, where sheer curtains swung in and out of an open window. Though it was mid-September, the rains held off, and the maple in the yard was already leafless, had already grown brittle. Today it looked like a spider web against the steely sky. Its lacy shadow moved on Matty's face, his head cocked to one side as if listening for something.

It is an art, sweeping with a baby on your hip, but Violet had it hard wired: pressure across his back with her left forearm as she gripped the handle. With her right hand lower down and swinging like a pendulum, she moved the straw bristles along wooden planks. She noticed that the planks had grown gray with weather and with time. Baby hugged her with his fat little thighs and kept a corner of her apron pulled up into his mouth, gummed into a small wad of cotton and saliva. The hem of the apron was lined with violets, a clever little thing she had picked up at the Five and Dime back in Conway. Inside the house, Ricky, her oldest, plucked at three strings of a miniature guitar, his hair greased by his own five year old hands to look like Johnnie Ray. He was destined never to learn to play, instead to become a pilot like his father, but for now he imagined himself on a stage with lights and a band like he had seen at the Arkansas County Fair that summer.

When Baby had crawled into the bathroom this morning, Ricky had put a dollop of Tres Flores pomade in his tuft of auburn hair, too, so that he looked like an even smaller Johnnie Ray, his smile as wide and his wail as ardent. Violet had laughed and kissed Ricky on the forehead, pushed the oily glob on Baby's head around a bit with her long fingers before scooping him into her arms. She had a "clairvoyant" hand, her neighbor Winona said. Winona had a book about palmistry that she pored over at night with a flashlight while the babies slept and her husband snored.

"Seems like hands got no need for clairvoyance," Violet had joked softly, turning her hand over to fan her long fingers with their white moon fingernails. But Winona had chided her for not taking it seriously.

"I mean it, Violet, there's a lot you could learn by studyin' yer' hand. Those pointy little fingers mean you're too sensitive. Like the world hurts you too much."

"Oh hush, Winona, you're scarin' the boys," she had said, but they hadn't been listening at all, Winona noticed. Violet had wiped her hands on a bright yellow apron and turned back to the dishes, while Winona puffed on a cigarette at the kitchen table, her glass of iced tea sweating on a corkboard coaster.

Now on the porch Violet sang softly to Baby in her husky alto. "If your heartaches seem to hang around too long," she crooned (he grinned around the drool and the apron still stuffed in his mouth), "and your blues keep getting bluer with each song, well remember sunshine can be found…" He laughed and patted her cheek with his free hand. "Oh Baby," she said then and grew quiet again. Matty, in the gossamer shadow of the maple's spindly branches, paused thoughtfully in his excavation, an indecipherable expression on his face as he regarded them. His brown corduroy jacket lined with shearling fleece, a hand-me-down from a child at one of the houses Violet had started cleaning in this past year, hung open over his white T-shirt, and both of the knees of his Carhartt pants were worn and caked with dirt. Baby paused, too, in his mastication of the corner of Violet's apron, and pointed a tiny finger at his brother, but as Violet took a broad stroke with the broom, he tipped and had to grab hold of her shoulder again so as not to fall from his perch.

Baby was named after the patron saint of soldiers. Silly, Violet thought, since she was not Catholic and did not come from Catholic stock. Sebastian. Violet had chosen it when Charlie had chosen to go to Korea. Charlie had laughed when she first spoke it. "Sounds like a Frenchman," he had said, that crooked smile emitting the name like it was a useless ornament, but not unkind. He was never unkind. Charlie had had his hands in her hair that night while they lay on the chenille bedspread (it was July-hot in November, she would recall later—strange). Charlie always loved her hair. Said it was like raven feathers. Like black smoke and silky. He had whispered the name into the mass of it that night, *Sebastian*, gently mocking his assent, as they had fallen asleep, the seed of their third boy just beginning to take shape in her swollen belly. The child was destined never to be called by his given name but instead the diminutive "Baby" that would "just stick" long after the years the name was fitting for his age.

But I invent all of this. It is the story I grow for myself in the absence of answers. I was seventeen when I built this part. Constructed it from the fantasy of love that had rooted itself in my heart as a young girl. I realized even then that it was as plausible as any other version of the truth that could be considered, though none of them was verifiable.

Violet could easily have been like this…before the change. From this to that. In an instant.

During my teenage-year visits, through the smoke of her cigarette, my grandmother responded only vaguely to my thoughtfully posed questions. They were not enough to penetrate the veil of her silence, the shadow of her solitude, cultivated by then for almost forty years. It was not enough that I was keenly interested in her story, which inevitably gave rise to my father's and to mine. Not enough that my deer-like eyes widened, dilated, to receive anything she might share, my body frozen like a doe listening for danger, any sign of life. When she pushed the long, brown cigarette into the little wooden spool that looked to me like a miniature barrel, that was the signal. The lilting smoke would clip itself and disconnect from the snubbed cigarette, rise into the air between us and vanish, and the conversation would end. Like that. *Like that.*

There was an eternity of failure and regret that populated the landscape of her life between this *dream memory* and the visits from her gangly granddaughter, decades later, that engendered it. Funny. Time is like that. Fluid, acrobatic. It is we, in our waking hours, who plant ourselves in a well conceived *now*, but in our sleep we travel its continuum and there become all the things we ever were, all the things we ever will be, spanning generations and the kaleidoscope of memory that lives us.

July 1988, Turlock, California

I sat on the couch, my feet tucked up under me, my father rigid in the arm chair between us, checking his watch and proclaiming in a low voice about the traffic that would delay us if we stayed too long, about the dog in the car, about by mom and brother across town at her sister's house, waiting to be picked up. Grandma Esther (I never called her Violet) puffed on her long, brown cigarette, tapping it into a fluted aluminum tray while the baseball game on the TV reflected blue in the lenses of her glasses. Her thin, gray hair was pulled into a ponytail at the back of her head, incongruously high like a cheerleader's, and tied 'round with a length of thick crafting yarn, pink or yellow. She wore a lounge set, which was the customary gift from my family on holidays, since mostly it seemed, she lounged. Never comfortably, though. My father's erect posture seemed inherited from his mother, who always sat bolt upright, never easing herself into the shape of the space she occupied.

Those visits were all the same, though we would be there in different configurations: my dad and me. My dad, my mother and me. My dad, my brother, me. The four of us. But always Grandma Esther, always my father, always my self. I would not miss one, convinced as I was that something would be revealed to me in the sliver of light shed on my paternal heritage by moments with Grandma Esther. My dad seemed to pant his way through those visits, trying not to fill his lungs with the smoke-filled darkness that pervaded Grandma Esther's little house in Turlock, California. It had never been his home. He had left her long before she moved into it with her third husband and their two daughters. How many half brothers and sisters was it now? He had forgotten, lost track. No--turned away.

I would scan her bookshelf, thirsty for understanding: a few classics, an almanac, some spy novels of which I had never heard. *Mein Kampf* was there, too, in German no less. My curiosity about this one would be forever unsatisfied. Some things I had the courage to ask about. Some things not. I romanticized that my grandmother was a closet intellectual. That she had taught herself German after high school, where she had dabbled in the foreign language as an elective course. That she had wanted to try to understand injustice and cruelty in their seminal stages and thus had acquired the book and pored over it in the months her husband was away, fighting against such sinister forces in the world (though in World War II, his first tour, he mostly flew utility missions, never saw "action" as it were).

There were knickknacks, too, in my grandmother's house. Little glass baubles, a matchbox car, stack of coasters ornamented with palm trees, snow globe from Wisconsin—a gift from a friend, for she had never been. And on the walls, what looked like contact paper or gift wrapping tissue, neatly arranged to cover the paint beneath it and punctuated by thumbtacks that held various useful items: a pair of scissors, a keychain, skein of yarn. I pictured Grandma Esther after we left, arranging herself on the couch there, all of these things in reach, a cigarette hanging from her dry lips. She would remain perfectly still for hours but with every little thing within her reach, including the remote of the television that murmured to her incessantly, the only company she had or wanted for weeks at a time.

When I tired of perusing the walls, I looked beyond them to the rectangle of light and color framed by the screen door and stepped into the poem again. It was an ongoing poem that came in fits and starts but always had at its center Grandma Esther, our strained exchanges, her lamp-lit cavern of a living room. The poem was always caged by the sonnet form, but with an extended line. I think it was for fear that the poem might otherwise spill messily across my mind (and the page). It might come off undisciplined and flabby, infused as it was by my urgency, my desire to know, my frustration at the silence that surrounded me. This way, when I started reeling and spewing my language like tears, the sonnet form whispered softly, "No, Meg, just here, just here," about the end of a line. "Just this sound, just this one," and I would know how to contain it, the story that breathed me.

On this day, I could see through the screen, there was a milk carton that had been fashioned into a birdhouse (by my grandmother?). It tilted precariously from the branches of the birch tree in the front yard. In the grass at the tree's roots, the roofed carton: white with red images, red words moving into each other at odd angles because of the cuts that had been made for the construction of the little house. I blinked my eyes and brought into focus a baby bird that was struggling to breathe, lying like an amputee with its wings pinned to its sides directly below the little house. The poem welcomed me as I entered…

Heritage

A bird lies in the crabgrass in the yard. It's so small
it could fit in the hollow of your throat, but you can
see that it's a jay. It has fallen twice: once from the tall
birch, softly wooded nest awkward, spreading like a fan

amid anemic branches. Once from the sky-colored
birdhouse where the neighbor set it, meaning to save
it from the local cats. Tiny bird balcony, cold
bed for a fledgling. Safe, she thought, and she gave

it a push away from the edge. Still, limp and wet
with birth, it pushed with small and crippled wings, not to fly
but to move heavily away from the birdhouse, from what
held it, might rescue it, and dropped like a too-honest reply.

It landed soundlessly, Violet curiously noting the special
stillness of fear, her cigarette smoking itself in its tray.

I would swim around in this language for long minutes that seemed endlessly protracted, only vaguely aware of my dad and grandmother speaking in low voices about the weather, an ailing "swamp cooler," plans to paint the outside of the house later in the summer when it had cooled some and the paint would not dry on the brush. These were the ways I saw my dad love Grandma Esther, who perhaps would not have received his love in any other form of expression. She did not seem to believe in it or to need it, and I often wanted to put my hand on his while we sat there and he tortured himself over his desire to flee, but it was not my way. I did not really see myself, my compassion, as legitimate, as *enough* on any level to provide him comfort. I was a mere child after all. *His* child, who had enjoyed all the benefits of a father building from scratch what was nonexistent in his own youth. What he had longed for and never had but which he knew was latent in him, some hereditary memory of care and consciousness, love and abundance. What did I know of suffering?

I could see that this desire to flee was the predominant feeling he had for the entire length of our thirty-five minute visit, and by the time we finally left, it had hardened in his throat: accusatory lump of guilt and anxiety. Grandma Esther was a hard woman who barely resembled the Violet I knew I had dreamed up but whom I believed, with every cell of me, existed somewhere in that transcendent space beyond time and separate from the suffering that cripples us. In my youthful optimism I believed in her love, and I believed that her sadness had leeched it from her life. It was like if I just sat in that living room long enough, the decorative orange balls of the afghan lining the couch tapping softly against my brown calves, I might discover it. In a look or a gesture. In a pause or an intonation. I did not.

September 1952, Bradford, Arkansas

When the black Lincoln Capri pulled up in front of the house, it sent a cloud of dust into the sky that was redolent of a miniature cyclone. Matty watched it as it lifted into the air and then plumed outward, until it was barely distinguishable from the dull sky behind it. He kept a peripheral watch on the men as they stepped out of the car and only tore his eyes from the sky when the dust was no longer visible. He slowly pressed his hands into the earth, packing the dirt into the space between his fingers and nails as he watched the men. He observed their rigid postures, their decorum, their meticulously uniformed bodies moving as if in slow motion toward his mother. She watched them too and just as slowly, collapsed into a soft little heap on the porch, Baby spilling away from her into the folds of her skirt. Bewildered, Baby collected himself and tried to climb her, but she was already wailing and crying, rocking in her insulated grief. Unaware of her boys. Unaware of the men.

It mattered not at all that the telegram declared Charlie Missing in Action. Every wife of an F-86 Sabre Jet pilot knew what that meant. For her, it was done and he was gone. For her boys, the same was true. Only it would happen over slow-moving time that they would lose their mother too. It mattered not at all that she was sitting right there before them in the huddle of apron and skirts and broom, her black hair falling along her brow like a raven's wing. She was gone. Matty turned back to his yellow bulldozer and with his voice made a mechanical kind of growling noise that swallowed his mother's low howl in his ears…

I'll be home before Christmas this year. It is a promise at the end of a letter about MIGS and F-86 missions and *Violet I miss you, I miss the boys, I saw a fire-orange star bend the blue of the sky and turn to ash, yesterday. Violet this is something I must tell you.* And then the silence that followed, worse than the tremulous sound of waiting. In the night she listened for the cricket's voice, but heard only the hollow music of herself. Hers was a song of fluid want, like gasoline on water, swirling away the end of an hour that became years. The black coral hair he loved became red then platinum, blond then auburn, until it was dull brown wisps tucked under various wigs, and the wanting became bitter, his name like a mackerel under her tongue. Grief cupped in her hand, the lisp of her life could barely be heard in the voices of her sons, even then beginning to fade, even then dissolving into memories of men.

There had been a radio transmission, and the report of a wingman who managed to survive the encounter with three, then six, then nine Russian MIGs along the Yalu River, and finally: silence. A vast sky void of evidence. Void of life. And no sign of Charlie or his plane. It had to happen all the time, Violet knew, and the officers seemed hopeful that he might be found. But her heart was like that sky, and though she sounded it again and again, she knew he was gone from her and would not return. It was an alarm that had gone up almost instantly when the car turned onto Roosevelt Road. Something about the way the clouds reflected in the windshield, about the way the dust swirled into the sky behind it before dissipating into dullness. No, she was already alone, hardly aware of the officers' masculine voices reaching her in waves across the infinite space that separated them. She felt the voices and understood their import, disembodied as they were from the words they formed, from the mouths that issued them. She intuited their content and the truths they carried, though it was not spoken that Charlie Carroll was likely dead, his body irretrievable.

Charlie had brothers back in Conway and Norfolk. Three of them, and they had all been pilots, too, had flown alongside their baby brother in World War II. They had a million stories of tussles with the enemy, of near misses, of miraculous escapes from the death that pursued them for the whole of that period. Russell had even been missing for two days once in the Aleutian Islands, some mix-up of communications, and had been found with a grin on his face and a cargo plane full of pale-faced soldiers. They had hitched a ride, not knowing how he liked to horse around. He had received a slap on the wrist for that stunt, and he remembered it fondly, told the story again and again at family gatherings. It could not have been that Russell really believed that such chicanery could be responsible for his brother's disappearance and this unwelcome news, but he betrayed no credence in the idea that Charlie had died that day along the border between North Korea and China.

The brothers were gentle with Violet on the phone, assured her that she must remain strong, must hold it together for her sons, but she had crumbled into a million pieces, and panic was already rising in her heart about how to live with three children and skill enough only to keep a house but not to pay for it. It is true that she had attended Arkansas State Teachers College with Charlie when they were courting, but as for so many girls, marriage had supplanted course work, and her major had shifted from Linguistics to Housekeeping and Childbearing...by correspondence, of course.

Violet had not felt repressed or robbed by this shift. In fact, she had been the envy of almost all the young women at ASTC in those days, enjoying the rapt attention and sole affection of the most handsome of the Carroll brothers. He was funny and smart, a tall drink of water with a glimmer in his caramel-colored eyes, and he was hers. A small church wedding and courtyard reception represented a million dreams of life and love that had floated around Charlie's ears as he moved through the halls and grounds of ASTC, young women hugging their books to their breasts and batting their eyelashes in his direction. But their efforts were futile, for his heart belonged to the dark beauty of his half-Cherokee bride, to her raven hair, to her Patti Page voice. To her sharp intellect and her ability to scold him gently in three different languages.

Violet had retained her books and would peruse them of an evening, once the babies were down and she could sit up in sweet solitude for as long as she could keep her eyes open. She would whisper the French phrases from Camus, the German lines of Rilke, the frozen ellipses of

Shakespeare. Her love for the written word was total, and once Charlie had left for the war, she would write him letter after letter in her ornate hand, and he would read and reread them, imagining the soft cadence of her voice in his ear. Their love grew exponentially in the space between correspondences. They say that absence makes the heart grow fonder, and when that absence has such linguistic gems from which to drape itself, the effect is intensified that much more. How she could describe the Arkansas sky on an August evening, the trees lifting their limbs in ecstasy to brush the underbelly of a blazing firmament. How she could convey the expression of one of their boys: in Ricky fervor, in Matty contemplation, in Baby Seb the sweetest devotion. Her language enraptured him and made it possible for Charlie to live one way on the earth and another in his waking dreams. Perhaps, she thought later, she had given him too much.

And how could the brothers have known? How could they have imagined a reality so different from their own? While their hopes fountained like fireworks, Violet's had been buried with the music of Charlie's letters, with the memory of his promises to return, to come back to teaching Physical Education in Bradford. Had she ever really believed in that version of future? How does one return, after all, to such a life after soaring as he had done, through two wars, limitation falling away like clouds, like *clouds*?

After World War II, there had been talk of jets, finally, and that was what had sent him beyond the horizon a second time. His longing had suffused the air in their little Arkansas home, and after several days of resisting, Violet had told him to go. F-86 Sabre Jets and the Korean War beckoned, and no amount of guilting him for deserting his own children or those many sweat-pant clad children of the Bradford rabble could serve to lessen his want. This, Violet knew, was all there was. She had learned early in life, from her own Indian mother and Irish father, that one does not ask another to rescind the dream in their heart. Not for love or family, not for obligation or faith. Sacrifices must be made at the source, else they be transformed into bitterness. Bitterness seeps into places that were meant for love but which yield themselves so easily to regret. *No*, she had told him, *You go, my darling. Fly.*

Chapter Two

April 1990, San Luis Obispo, California

In April of 1990 I was a freshman in college. I had spent the year undoing a lifetime of wholesomeness and piety, exploring every variety of alcohol and even one Ziploc baggie of shake that resulted in about three hours of paranoid fretting. Something had struck me upon entering school three hundred miles down the coast from my hometown: *I can reinvent myself here. I can be anything I want.* It was a relief, really, after having been locked in to the prudish image of myself that I had projected throughout high school. I had been restraining myself for so long that it had seemed too strange, too odd, to do otherwise in the company of those who had always known me. But here... *Here.*

I remember walking onto campus for the first time, tucked into rolling green hills and surrounded by the one hundred seventeen mountain peaks that are included within San Luis Obispo's topography. It felt still, static compared with the open coastline of Northern California. But it also felt comfortable, nourishing, like a nest there at the mouth of Poly Canyon, which cradled Brizziolari Creek as it meandered its way from the Northeast and opened onto the rodeo grounds and corrals of the school's environs. I had been invited to "rush," and because I had never heard of the Greek system and could not fathom the appeal of a voluntary social structure that would require from me both money and the wearing of dresses, I passed, preferring instead the freedoms of life as a "surfer girl." Morro Bay was only about fifteen minutes to the north, Los Osos National Park only about twenty minutes to the south. Both served as open playgrounds where I could pass my time enveloped in dark water, breathing marine air, wearing the salty residue of sessions spent in the freezing Pacific Ocean, searching and riding waves.

I had spent my younger years being painfully good. I was a Christian girl, sang in the choir, traveled to Mexico to help build houses, the whole nine. I was performance oriented, a straight-A student, an elite athlete, and competitive to the nth degree. In my black-and-white thinking there was really no abstraction, no gray area in which I could flounder or equivocate. When the elders of my church read from the scriptures and said that young women should strive to "be like Mary," I did not hesitate.

"I can do that," I honestly thought, and I did. I was as straight-laced as an eighties girl could be, aside from the fact that in high school I had stopped wearing underwear for the sake of convenience. Not so that I could be promiscuous but so that I could be efficient in my "deck changes" from sweat pants and UGG boots to wetsuit, for I was already an avid surfer then, and this was how my guy friends did it. I spent hours and hours in the ocean, devoting whole days to finding waves, riding them, warming up over chai tea and paddling out again. I would clench slick auburn bulbs of seaweed in my hands, pull myself tirelessly through kelp webs to find my way into a lineup of boys who loved the sea as I did. Who listened to her with as intent an ear and believed as I did that she moved for us alone.

I was full of contradictions, but a few things were certain: I did not drink, I did not smoke, and I did not "put out." This latter piece had complicated my various "relationships" in high school and in that first fall of college. While I immediately allowed my dorm mates to introduce me to alcohol (I believe Southern Comfort was their choice for my indoctrination), I maintained my piety around sexual activity, and though I must have kissed a dozen boys by the time I met Adrian, I never gave myself away, never doffed my clothing, never lost my virginity, such as it was.

Adrian scooped me one drunken night from a wild party where I was likely to have been violated had I stayed there alone (I quail to think of the positions I put myself in during those chaotic days, how many times I only narrowly escaped the kinds of traumas that one does not easily absorb). He drove me out to Avila Beach in my own pickup, and though I recall almost nothing from that night, I do remember him looking at me like one looks at a kitten who has misbehaved, or a small child, enamored and only barely reproachful. He held me that night like I was a jewel, like I was something special, though I had lost all grace and was, quite frankly, barely conscious. He kissed me tenderly, and that was all. There was probably some thrill in having me like that, so vulnerable, and not acting. Who can tell, but I was grateful for Adrian's restraint and for being tucked into bed fully clothed, only my shoes gently removed and placed next to my raised dormitory bed.

My relationship with Adrian grew out of the imbalance of our personalities, forging a kind of unlikely wholeness for a time. Adrian was funny. He was short-sighted at best and never seemed to take anything seriously. All of this was in sharp contrast to my seriousness about life. Yes, I had grown into the habit of blowing the top off the weekends, but as a student I was extremely focused and diligent, and about many things I never joked. I spent most of my free time in the sea, cleansing myself of the residue of nights that shamed me, separated me from that Mary-like standard and thrust me into the confusion of identity that comes for us all at one point or another. I still have suspended memories of being lifted on salt water as swells drove along beneath me and I scanned the horizon for the perfect wave. Perfection was the problem, of course, but it would be many years before I could get my head around that. I still believed then that perfection could be achieved, not only intended but actually manifested. Where moral attitudes are concerned, this is among the most dangerous of ideas, certainly among the most self-destructive.

My bulimia raged in those days, and at intervals I would make the small pilgrimage over to the on-campus health center when it got "out of hand," like when I started using the handle of a hairbrush, because my gag reflex had become insensitive to my probing index finger. I was a strong girl with thighs like a sprinter, though I had never been a runner. My waist was disproportionately small for my generous hips, my stomach perfectly flat, but my shoulders were broad, supported as they were by a surfer's deltoids. This was all at odds with my desire to look like Kate Moss, with whom the only quality I shared was my small breasts. Perhaps as a punishment to myself, I cut the bangs of my black hair, the most beautiful trait I had inherited from Violet, in a straight, severe line well above my eyebrows. The athletic female had yet to make its way into the media as a model for beauty, and in my infinite perfectionism, my lack of imagination and generosity toward myself had naturally grown into the eating disorder that had plagued me by then for two years. I punished myself in many ways, and to my father's chagrin, I refused to grow out my absurd little bangs in favor of a softer, more feminine look.

Adrian, however, seemed to find me exquisite. Though that first night I probably reeked of alcohol and cloves (another foray into the contraband), was sloppy drunk and foolishly rambling about God knows what, he beheld me as one beholds a surprise gift. His eyes held in them some other-worldly light, and I was dimly captivated. His hair was as black as mine but fell in loose curls above his eyes. His skin was fair and punctuated by a fine smattering of freckles. His body was lanky and long, so that he moved with a fluidity and ease that reminded me at once of Dorothy's Scarecrow and of a dancer I had seen in a movie once. Like at times he had no bones, like he could move with any change life grew in his path. Like he could wrap himself around me and protect me from all the ways I was constantly hurting myself. His laughter was full and rich, and I knew it had the power to heal me, though I often resisted it, often turned away from the silliness that was most of the time inconvenient or incongruous with what I felt I had to say or do.

Looking back, I think he knew he was going. That soon he would lift off, leave me there on the tilting earth we had walked together for only eight months. In April of 1990, while on one continent an American businessman was discovering my grandfather Charlie Carroll's dog tags in a Chinese war museum, raising new questions about his never-explained disappearance, Adrian was making plans to go to the quarry with Roddy and Ben. Somewhere—Russia?

China?— an investigation was beginning, re-opening into the possibilities of a thirty-seven year-old anomaly: a pilot and his Sabre jet absorbed into blue sky, like that. *Like that.*

My sixty seven year old grandmother barely raised an eyebrow when she got this news, but then she never betrayed any emotion and left me to invent it: a beat of her heart missed, sharp inhalation of stale air, distant recollection of hope regained and lost in an instant--*Oh*! And here, here in my corner of the universe, my relationship was fractured and, without my knowledge (might I have seen it, had I been attuned?), Adrian was moving toward a light I barely believed in any more.

It was an abandoned rock quarry, filled with water dark as pitch, that had closed many years before and was little known. The place offered various levels of harrowing adventure to the willing jumper. It was illegal, of course, dangerous as it is to leap from such great heights into water that is mysterious and still and deeper than anyone is willing to dive. It would involve cruising up to the outskirts of the quarry around five in the morning with headlights off, scrambling over a chain link fence and walking a quarter of a mile to the site of the pit. I wanted nothing to do with it and would not even share in the discussion of plans.

Adrian and I had decided to "give it a rest" after a long conversation in my dorm room, my puritanical standards at odds with his free-spirited lifestyle and his sexual prime. I remember he wondered about the timing of it, meeting me then when he was most desirous of freedom and adventure, when five years hence, he thought, it would have been perfect. There was that word again. Five years away from *perfect.* Tough, I had thought, and I said it, too. *Tough shit.*

There was a girl, too. From his hometown. Marie is the name I've given her—or that I remember? She was not going to college, not pursuing higher education at all, but she was beautiful and funny and in love with him. I suspected she was giving Adrian what I was not, but in our agreement to separate, I had decided it was not my business. I had even convinced myself that I did not care. I had seen a single photograph of her. She wore heavy eyeliner in sharp contrast to my barefaced countenance; I rarely wore eye makeup, unless there was no chance I would find my way into the ocean on a given day, which was pretty much never. Her smile was pretty, slightly asymmetrical, and she had deep dimples on either side of her puckered mouth.

Marie had bleached out the ends of her hair, probably some home dye job, but I had a feeling that she never criticized Adrian for being silly, never asked of him anything he could not deliver. I had the distinct feeling that precisely those things that drove me crazy about him, how he never seemed to plan for his future, never took seriously those things that I contemplated deliberately and with no small amount of agitation (the meaning of things, the language we give them, the shape a life can take); these were the very things about Adrian in which Marie delighted. Five years from now, I thought, Marie would have used him up perhaps, but then maybe he would be ready for me. For my somber respect for life. This is how I saw it.

The last time I was with Adrian, I had walked past him and a mutual friend named Adam. In my awkwardness, my utter inability to inhabit my own skin comfortably and in light of the recent shift in our relationship, I did not greet them. I remember Adam scoffing as I passed. I imagine Adrian had said something like, "Watch this, she won't even say 'hello'," and I did not disappoint. My vitals would not calm, my breath find its way into a greater passageway than my clenched throat had offered it, until I was safely inside the glass doors of my dormitory. How had it come to this?

Later that night Adrian would visit me in my dorm room. It would be uncomfortable, but he would not flinch. He would hold my gaze longer than I could bear, pick up little items from my desk—a framed photo of my parents, a stone I had collected from Waddell Creek up North, a lavender-scented candle. He would turn each over in his hand, comment, laugh softly again.

"What?" I wanted to know, though there was nothing but ease in his manner. He would ask me for a shoulder massage and would lean against my cinder-block-raised bed to receive it. Only half grudgingly I would rub his shoulders, while Wilson Phillips crooned on my stereo. Probably a homemade cassette, though I had begun to collect CDs. We stayed that way for what seemed like an interminable period, and I will never forget Adrian's voice as he whispered the words of a song's chorus: "Release me," he said, his voice full of breath. "Release me." It sent a serpentine coil of fear and strangeness up my spine, I recall, but I had rationalized it. *Yes*, I had thought. *Perhaps it is time to let you go*. That was the last time we spoke.

I came back to school after a weekend away the next Sunday evening, and it was Norma Calvert who met me at the door of Mo's. Her pallor and her melodramatic greeting set me only slightly on edge. As usual, I paid Norma no mind, but I would later remember how some part of me registered the sea of faces beyond her, who seemed also to look on in anticipation. I would recall dismissing this, too, as I made my way through the heavy double doors and situated myself at the bar to order a basket of fries. Norma was relentless, though. She approached me with her breasts pushing up towards her chin, as they always were, sequestered in the underwire effort of her bra, its black lace just visible over the top of her low-cut shirt. Incongruously, she wore her dirty blond hair pulled into two partial pigtails on either side, though *Mork and Mindy,* the show that had been the advent of the style, had stopped running nearly ten years before. *Meg should know*, Norma reasoned to herself, *and I should be the one to tell her.* And just like that, the poem again became the only safe place to inhabit.

Strange the way Meg reacted when Norma told her the news,
Adrian sinking to the bottom instead of floating to the top: she
ran onto the slanting lawn in front of Mo's, said she had to choose
a star to carry in her throat, let one sandal dangle crazily

from her ankle, brown leather strap binding broken shoe to body.
Her wild prayers spilled into the air and tangled themselves in

the whine of freeway traffic: a long and braided treaty
with the god of her dreams. She spun around then, her thin

neck stretching with the points of the swallowed star. She pressed
strange fists into her stomach, into her breasts, looked to Norma
crying in the doorway of Mo's but could only see the light that dressed
Norma's body there. *Save me.* She sent the words to form a

ring around the hole where her star had been, but they fell on
the grass beside her. The bouyancy in the air was already gone.

Adrian was already gone by the time I learned of the accident at the quarry. Though there had been no brain activity by the time they had fished him from the dark water and spirited him to the hospital in Paso Robles, they had kept him on life support most of the day. By the time I called to the hospital, there was no one to speak to. No one to explain or appease my rising panic, for even then I did not know that his spirit had long since lifted itself from the failing shell that was Adrian's body. I did not know that Adrian's spirit had hovered, gentle, gentle, over his parents as they spoke with a chaplain and were counseled to let him go, disconnect machine from mortal coil. To let his body fall away from what was less dense, less substantial, but more real than could be imagined…and they had. And he had slipped away during the hours that I had driven along the coast on my way home, wholly unaware. Unattuned, as had been my habit in those last weeks before he made his exit.

It would take the keen attunement of grief for me to recognize the many signs he had given me, even in his boy-man-consciousness. Surely he did not really know that he would die, not on a conscious level, but there seemed to me certain hints and instances that would have held little meaning had they not added up, finally, to the prelude to his departure. I felt that I was tumbling incredulously, almost weightlessly, in the anachronism of it all: me learning too late (for what, I wonder now?) that Adrian was gone, being precisely two hours behind his parents and sister in their grieving (making panicked phone calls while they were somewhere else, holding each other and weeping their good byes), of the thing itself (a boy dying before his mother). *Oh.*

And the loss changed the relationship. Now it was perfect. And so was Adrian. Even *I* was lovely in my reminiscence. Every frustration was now an endearment, had I had the presence of mind to perceive it. Every irresponsible, every impetuous act was now evidence of an exuberance that I had always lacked and for which I would now always long. Risking life and limb to skateboard the harrowingly steep asphalt path from the top of campus to the library lawn sans helmet or even long pants was now a banner of his free spirited whimsy, not an expression of his lack of concern for me and for others who loved him. Falsifying his university report card was no longer the last straw in a series of acts that evidenced the chasm between our realities. Along with all the other things, it became a secret message about seizing the moment, about Adrian's mystical foreboding that had ignited in him not fear but a fine frenzy of love and desire...and of course a sequence of insufferable shenanigans that would result in our "break up" only two weeks before his death.

That same spring, somewhere in a village south of Dandong, China a penjing artist named Zhang Min had unknowingly built a studio over the exact coordinates of a Korean War crash site. Coordinates that had never been revealed but would eventually be disclosed as part of an agreement between the U.S. and Russian governments. The two countries would, for the first time since the 19th century, share archived information that might illuminate the cases of soldiers missing from as far back as World War I, and those who had ever been prisoners of war. While my world was collapsing in on itself, while I was effectively shrouding myself in the grief that was only marginally mine to bear, a Chinese man was framing up a space and filling it with cutters, trimmers, soil and pots of all varieties, all in service of his craft. This studio with its high windows would bury even more deeply the truth about my grandfather's life and death, until one day it would yield itself to an archaeological dig and reveal the very pith and marrow of that truth. But not yet. Not yet.

Chapter Three

January 1954, Bradford, Arkansas

When the officer arrived to confirm that Charlie had in fact been declared Killed in Action, though no further evidence of his body or aircraft had emerged in the fifteen months following his disappearance, he knocked gently on the door of Violet's house. It was darkened and quiet, but he had seen a boy in the yard; the boy had been wearing cowboy boots and hitting a tire swing with a stick. The officer assumed that the child was not home alone, as he could only have been three or four years old, so he shifted his weight on his feet and knocked a second time. The papers in his hands trembled slightly, the only evidence of his uneasiness. These visits were never fun, and small waves of nausea moved over him as he waited. He could see that there was movement in the house now, quiet rustling, a disembodied lamp lighting itself from behind the white curtains.

At the door, Violet looked strange, not the same woman who had been standing on the porch just over a year ago, singing Jimmie Ray songs to a child in her arms. That woman had been full of life, had exuded a kind of warm sensuality, though it had shattered into her grief before he and his colleague had even reached her. That woman had hair that was as black as the onyx stones set in the Indian jewelry he had bought his own wife earlier that year. That woman had worn a dress, he thought, and garnet colored lipstick. How clear his memory had become standing here waiting for her to open the door, distilled as it was by time and by his own apprehension. How strange that when we wait in stillness, our worlds reassemble themselves from the chaos of our unmemory.

The woman he could see through the fibers of a screen door now had red hair, unnaturally red, and she wore a housedress and slippers, though it was after noon. She was thin and her brown skin had grown pale; a cigarette dangled from between her index and middle fingers. "Mrs. Esther Carroll?" he queried.

"Mrs. Blake," she corrected.

"Uh, I'm looking for Esther Carroll, please?"

"I'm Esther Blake," she said through a drowsy haze. "Remarried. What can I do for you?" It was awkward, to say the least. There was no precedent for this, and the officer blanched, considering how to deliver news that was obviously obsolete, or at least irrelevant: the official Army declaration of her first husband's death. It seemed silly, even to him just then, that this news had been produced by nothing more than the passage of time: MIA to KIA in the standard space of a year. And here was the woman who had received both letters, nearly unrecognizable from his first visit, clearly wearing a wedding band (could it be the same one?). He recognized the young child at her side, maybe eighteen months old now, as the baby from that strangely still September day. The baby had clung to her skirts then, and he clung to her housedress now, a clear gloss of snot spreading above his upper lip.

The officer had slipped the letter through the small slot Violet made by pushing the screen door open just enough, and he waited for her to read it. When her gaze met his again, it was cold and level, no longer drowsy in the least. He thought of several things to say, rejected them all, and waited for her to speak. When she did not, he parted his lips twice, as if to form words, thought better of it and turned to go in silence. He wiped his sweating hands on his pant legs as he descended the porch steps, careful to miss the one that appeared to be broken. At the bottom of the stairs, which felt like an infinite distance, he turned back to her and raised his hand slightly, again as if to speak. She was still standing there watching him, the hand with the letter on her hip, almond-shaped eyes narrowing and cheeks sucking inward as she took another long, slow drag on the cigarette.

He could feel the simmer of her attention on his back as he moved away from the house and its heaviness. He would carry that weight with him for some time, though he had never known Charlie Carroll, never exchanged words with his wife except to announce his absence, both ostensible and confirmed. And by what right had he delivered these military declarations? Where indeed was Robert Charles Carroll? He had been absorbed into a blue sky over the Yalu River, it seemed (MIA?). Soundless and still, neither the sky nor the river valley below it had yielded any sign of him in the days following his last mission. The officer had read the reports. It was as if there was a hole in the universe, and man and jet had been sucked through it that day, leaving no trace (KIA?). Here in Bradford, Arkansas: the remains of a life that had been sweet. Settled and honest. But now, in its place…this. Is beauty so dependent on love? The boy under the tree positioned the tire swing between himself and the car as it drove away, leaving no dust this time but rather two shallow tire track trenches in the saturated dirt road.

Violet gave a cursory glance in the direction of Matty, who was still watching the car recede, and then she closed the door. It was Matty's habit to stay out of doors most of the day. When it got too cold or dark, he would come inside and read books with the flashlight he had gotten for Christmas the year his daddy did not come home. There was little privacy in the small house where Matty shared a bedroom with his two brothers, but he had hung a sheet over a cotton clothesline to form a sort of tent over his bed.

There he would spend hours immersed in fictions that swept him up and away from his Bradford home and the loveless drawl of his vacant-eyed mother. He loved her, and he found her beautiful, even as changed as she was, but he could not get near her, he found, and the more time that passed, the less it seemed possible even to touch her hand.

That was also the year that Ricky and Matty found out about Santa, because there were no presents when they woke up. They had been delivered later by Uncle Lawrence and Uncle Eddie, dressed as Santa Claus. "Look who I found wandering around outside!" Uncle Lawrence had proclaimed to the boys, his hands on his knees in the doorway. Uncle Eddie had leaned into the doorframe then, his long white beard attached at the ears and falling onto Uncle Lawrence's shoulder.

"Ho, ho, ho!" he had bellowed jovially, entering with a sack over his shoulder. From the sack he had fished a package for each boy and one for Violet, but it was not enough to penetrate the sadness that year. Even the uncles seemed a little out of sorts despite their best effort, and these things do not usually go unnoticed by children. That Christmas was supposed to have been spent with Charlie after his last F-86 mission, and the expectation of that still hung in the air like smoke. Uncle Eddie had played Bing Crosby's "White Christmas" on the old phonograph, but the ground outside was hard and brown, frozen solid with hoarfrost. Violet retired to her room and left the boys to play card games with Uncle Lawrence and Uncle Eddie, who had given up the charade and wore his beard below his chin like an elaborate white scarf. Aunt Bernice had arrived an hour later with a ham and spent the afternoon baking it and preparing a Christmas meal, the last the boys would have together under their mother's roof.

Faltering now and leaning against the closed door, Violet closed her eyes and blew the cigarette smoke from her lungs into the room. The officer had gone without saying a word. He had looked surprised when she said she was remarried, but that had been all. She still held the letter in her hand, but she would not open it again to read the words to which she attached no meaning. It would be some time before Dennis would come home from the factory, Violet knew, but she was up now and might as well get dressed. She dropped the paper in the trashcan and opened the refrigerator door: a half a bottle of orange juice and four eggs. She called Ricky to do the morning chores, but they had already been done. The older boys had already eaten toast with peanut butter and dressed themselves and Baby before she rose. She washed the few dishes that were in the sink and drank a glass of orange juice by herself.

Another year and even this level of obligatory posturing would be abandoned. Violet would stop pretending to monitor the children's activities at all, so that Uncle Lawrence would come and take the boys back to Conway with him for the summer…to give her a chance to pull herself together, he would say.

One Year After the Telegram

Her heart has slipped down her left leg, a free
agent now, settled in her heel. Beating
still. Moving the blood. Stirring it. And she
will sleep with Dennis tonight. Something

about him that's not so hard. She sees her
self floating in his irises, sees her
self shudder under his climax. Sees her
body flatten under his weight and then

lift itself on the wave of unmemory,
un-consciousness, wave of a sigh. Moments
gone, just like that. Nothing in their place. She
opens her hibiscus lips and says, "O," has rent

the letters into pieces, reassigned them.
Moribund Insomniac Azaleas.

July 1955, Bradford, Arkansas

Uncle Lawrence sneered at her when he came for the boys that summer in his Ford pickup the color of Montana sky. He and Uncle Eddie loaded the bags into the back of the truck and lined the boys up between them on the bench seat. Violet could see that the two men hated her. Despised her for the hope she had never indulged but which each of the brothers still carried under his tongue. Charlie had been dead for nearly three years now, but they had never believed it. There was even talk of Russian MiGs forcing American pilots out of the sky during the Korean War and taking them back to Russian soil to be interrogated about American aviation technology. Perhaps Charlie was living there even now, they speculated, amnesiac or still being held against his will. Violet's refusal to embrace such wild hopes, and her precipitous marriage to a factory worker named Dennis Blake, had turned them from her.

The brothers would have denied her all together if it had not been for the boys, each of them a whisper of Charlie's existence, each of their faces encapsulating a vivid memory of love and brotherhood. Baby, who was three now and getting old to be called that, was small for his age and would ride on Uncle Eddie's knee most of the way to Conway, tugging at his ears and fiddling with the buttons on his shirt. At one point the two older brothers would be allowed to sit in the bed of the truck, as long as they stayed up against the cab, eating the dipped cones Uncle Eddie had bought them at a roadside dairy bar. Warm air on their skin and in their hair, along with the sweet sensation of vanilla ice cream on their tongues, was exhilarating and would make them believe, if only for a moment, in something good, perhaps just around the next corner. Such is the resiliency of childhood.

Violet stood in the open doorway of her house for an hour after Uncle Lawrence's pickup departed, letting the swamp cooler run uselessly. She was trying to remember something she had forgotten, was paralyzed by its elusiveness. Once while she stood there, she pushed an errant strand of hair, blond this time, behind her ear. Otherwise, she was completely still, her lips parted almost imperceptibly to admit her languid breath. When Dennis Blake came home (he had made himself scarce to avoid another confrontation with the ex-brothers-in-law) he yelled at his wife for wasting power, for making a spectacle of herself again. Two boys in striped shirts had stopped on their bikes to observe the beautiful ghost in the doorway (*Was she frozen?* they would have wondered if it had not been for the heat). Dennis yelled at them, too, and sent them skidding down the dirt lane. Then he shuffled Violet roughly inside and slammed the door shut. He cracked a beer and sat down in the vinyl-upholstered easy chair, listening to the radio with his eyes closed while Violet disappeared into the bedroom for the rest of the day.

Lying on her bed, Violet cupped her small breasts in her hands and in this way experienced her breathing from the outside. Thin now with the waste of grief and self-denial, Violet nearly disappeared beneath the sheath of a dress she wore. Tears soaked her temples and made invisible rivulets along her scalp as she lay there beneath the cracked plaster of her bedroom ceiling, so that finally her pillow became wet with her longing. But she was not foolish enough to call it that, because for what does one long when her tall drink of water lover, the tender father of her children, clever anchor in the inundating sea of her life, disappears through a hole in the universe, bends the blue sky around himself and goes to sleep for good?

Her soft moaning eventually turned into words, and she began to sing quietly in that space. "Now give me once more that kiss I adore,/ Then I'll let you go just for now," she intoned softly, her vague prayers to Charlie (never to God) taking the shape they always did: that of a popular music song. Today, as always, they seemed to get lost in the space between her lips and the ceiling. "But we'll meet again, another time,/ Another place, I know…"

When Violet woke from her sleep several hours later, Dennis would be gone. No note or explanation, just a vague absence where he had occupied space before. She would shuffle through the house for a while, straightening things: a doily on the back of a chair, the salt and pepper shakers on the table (they were in the shapes of New Hampshire and Vermont, a souvenir from Aunt Bernice who had traveled there), a pair of shoes by the front door. Touching this or that: a snow globe, the dusty top of the radio, a cloudy mirror that hung on the wall. Adjusting things: thin curtains, the floral area rug, her own unruly hair. Then she would sit down where her husband of nearly two years had been, next to the radio, and listen to a litany of pop songs until she fell asleep again, subsiding into the only reprieve she knew. Violet would not tell Dennis about the twins until after they were born the following spring, but even that would not bring him back to her and to her boys, who would return from their summer with Uncle

Lawrence a little plumper, a little cleaner and a little less afraid.

Chapter Four

May 1992, San Luis Obispo, California

I was a train wreck after Adrian died. For a long time. I think that it had to do with the fact that what had happened to him was so inconsistent with what I thought I believed. About God. About faith and prayer. About the world beneath heaven. The structure of the belief system that I had built around me like a stained glass cathedral, which I had always thought kept me safe, even from my own self-loathing, shattered the day that Adrian died. The pieces, blue and red, purple and gold, flew apart, blew themselves to the four corners of the earth, leaving me naked and without shelter. I thought, with good reason, that those pieces could not be recovered.

In those early days, I sought solace in every imaginable place, even the Catholic Church. The local congregation met in the Mission San Luis Obispo de Tolosa downtown, and my friend Kristina sang in the choir. The Mission is beautiful with its white stucco walls and Spanish-tile roof. The curvy numbers 1772 adorn the front of the building, indicating the year of its founding under the direction of Father Junipero Serra, who had founded four others like it along the California coast. A fountain adorns the grounds in front of the church now; bronze statues of three bears, a mother and her cubs, appear to play in its waters, alongside a bronze Chumash Indian girl. She sits next to the bears, apparently unaware or disbelieving of any danger that being in such close proximity to bears might present, her feet dipping into the cool waters of the moving pool. Sporting traditional couture, the girl has bangs cut straight across and high on her forehead.

Sundays, I would go to evening mass to hear Kristina sing and to be enveloped in the ritual of the service. Stand up, sit down, kneel, chant, keep silent. I loved the decorum and the sanctity of shared rites. I was always a step behind, but I followed along, murmured my assent or repetition when appropriate, but knew not to take my place in line for the Eucharist.

When I went to see him in his compartment, a doughy, red-faced priest listened to me patiently, as I related to him the story of my sadness, of my shattered faith-cathedral. I accepted the tissues as he fed them to me across his desk, one at a time. When I was finished speaking, my face flushed and wet with tears, it must have been perfectly clear that what I sought was simply a spiritual home. A place to lay down my resistance to grace. The priest's face seemed understanding and gentle, even with the beaded sweat across his bare upper lip, but he began to shake his head slowly. An alarm broke loose in my ribcage then, because I sensed the impending rejection. He broke it to me regretfully that should I choose to convert now, I would always be a "stepchild" in the congregation. He spent a fair amount of time explaining how arduous a process it would be to convert to Catholicism and for, in the end, imperfect results.

It is so strange what some people will do with power and structure. How they cannot see beyond either of those things to find their way to human compassion, even where it is most desperately needed. I left the priest's office bewildered and still crying that day. I did not go back. Years later I would learn to separate religious ideologies from the human beings who serve as their vehicles, inadequate as we all are for the bearing of perfection. Ideas and even language can be perfect, I learned, but people never can. This was a lesson that took many years to absorb.

I sought solace in alcohol, too, which was short lived, as I had already been that way. I quickly found that the ephemeral hours of numbness and disconnection from what ached like teeth along my spine did not warrant the period of raw pain and nausea that inevitably followed them. I sought solace in asceticism, as well. I denied myself every good thing and would run for miles and miles on open roads, pounding my bones against asphalt while my head swam in its distress, my breath chafing ragged and strange in my ears. I sought it in writing. I produced volumes of self-indulgent blather that had therapeutic value perhaps, but not literary merit. Franz Kafka once said that writing is a form of prayer. These were my disillusioned prayers, akin to Violet's songs, to Adrian and not to God, both of whom had forsaken me and disappeared. I "spoke" to Adrian bitterly, denying God with my words as I had done with my heart.

I spent my days listening to music with headphones, which provided an automatic barrier between myself and anyone who might approach me. I was a ghost moving through campus, sitting in classes, taking copious notes about the rise of the Cold War, the influence of the Romantic poets on the Victorians, the philosophies of Heidegger and Kierkegaard. I gathered language and thought to me, hoarded it all in my heart, reconstructed and spun it into new syntaxes on exams and in essays. And to what end? Perhaps it was all part of my effort never to be still. Never to be alone with my actual thoughts, my real sensations, at least until night fell and I could recede from the throngs of people that populated campus. Never did I feel more alone than when I was surrounded by all that chatter. So many lives going on simultaneously, independently, seemingly separate and ultimately, it occurred to me, solitary. It was a thought that was for me full of despair.

Every night I would climb to the flat roof of the red brick science building and recline beneath night skies blooming with constellations. I would breathe the cool air and listen to the nothing that filled it. Occasionally I could hear the movement of people, their hollow voices below me on the walking paths, coming back from town or from a late session at the library. A hollow laugh rising skyward, a conversation in voices lowered to a murmur. A joyful whoop into the night. But those voices felt small and far away, pretend people floating in the ether of my star-filled life. Mostly it was silent.

In May of 1992 I was enrolled in a seminar on Albert Camus, the French existentialist and father of the Absurd. In Camus' world, the universe is indifferent to the individual, and though we long inherently for meaning in our lives, the universe cannot and will not provide it. The best we can do is accept what is, declare as Sophocles' Oedipus did that "all is well." One looks back on her life and recognizes her present moment as the culmination of a million little choices she made, freely and without any sort of divine intervention (for what *is* the divine, Camus might ask, but an invention of a mind desperate to construct meaning in the meaningless arena of our existence?). It has to be that we are solely responsible for what comprises our experience, for what is life but a sequence of actions dictated by individual choice? The exercise of free will. Herein lay the conflict in my mind. Though I could cognitively accept these things as true, they wholly denied the existence of the divine, and though it was true that I felt abandoned by God, I was not ever really willing to believe that he (she?) did not exist.

Could it have been my own choices that had led me here, to this supreme anguish? It felt as I lay there on the science building roof that my heart had split open, that all those stars were spilling from my body in a wild rush of my own desire, splitting and multiplying like cells as they hit the cool night air. That *desire*, I think, was to have the intensity of my emotion, both pleasurable and torturous, validated somehow. Transformed into something alive and bright and real in this world. I wanted it to be made into something meaningful. It seemed impossible, though, and I lacked the direction to achieve such a transformation. I even lacked the clarity to envision it, but in that nebulous suffering I think it is fair to say I hoped.

Camus, and even the Buddhists I later discovered, would say that it was my hope that tormented me. Had I, at any point, been able to accept what was mine, I might have healed: a boy with a mischievous smile and a numinous light in his eyes—for precisely eight months. All of those months were preserved in my mind and admittedly sweetened with their temporality. If I could have accepted that time as *all*, as enough, and relinquished the hope for something more than numbness, I could have moved forward into the next phase of my life with some degree of grace. It is that human tendency to grasp, to want more than is given, that ruins us. But perhaps it is also what saves us.

In the end, I could not accept Camus' declaration of the 'indifference of the universe' and the hollow nothing that returned to me as I lay there on that rooftop, softly moaning my sadness into the air. If I ascribed to Camus' philosophy, the silence with which the universe responded was not only a function of its size, which was obviously too vast to return an echo, but also of its dearth of compassion, its lack of any divine entity to animate it and hear my supplication. I was attracted to Camus' intellectual sureness, his confidence in his own devastating conclusions, but I could not succumb to his hopelessness. As for Buddhism, which I was only beginning to explore, acceptance of temporality seemed like a facile tenet, but to view the death of someone I had loved, the death of a child before his mother, as simple change...I knew myself as incapable of such thought. It is possible, after all, to intellectually grasp something and at the same time be wholly incapable of producing the matching sentiment.

Though I was not willing to test it, I secretly guarded the seed of hope that slept in my heart, and I protected it against what felt to me like unadulterated cynicism. Camus' philosophy seemed a sinister denial of what I wanted to believe in: the inherent connection among all things, living and inanimate. I picked from each belief system what I could embrace and began to build a new spiritual structure around myself. This one would be equally beautiful but perhaps constituted of stronger stuff: brick and mortar, plaster and wooden beams.

The universal *Om* was a bright little light in my interior sky. The darkness of that sky had not failed to mute every other light that emerged, but the idea of the transcendent *all*, the divine dissolution of the membranes, the walls and chasms that separated us from one another…I wanted to believe in that. I wanted to believe in something superhuman. Something numinous and supernal and which transcended the human mire of grieving. *If only one could perceive it, embrace it with her life.*

In the first years after Adrian died, I saw myself as having been cut from a critical umbilicus that had once joined me to that *Om*, to the rest of humanity. Now, the remnant of that cord hung loose from my body, purposeless and shrunken. Eventually, I thought, if I let it, all evidence of such a connection would disappear completely, leave a neat little seal where that lifeline had been. I felt myself as floating through space, listless astronaut having lost the blueprint for her exploration and instead navigating the arbitrariness of uncharted stars. But by May of 1992 I knew, somewhere in my seemingly vacuous consciousness, that it was up to me not to allow that severed connection to become permanent. I knew that this would destroy me and that somehow this *would* be a result of my own choosing. Thus, I held on, if only tenuously and between bouts of illusion, to the real.

Layered with my philosophical contemplations was what I could only identify as sheer fear. It felt cold as it moved along my spine and inside my skull, and I knew it intimately. Though I was not conscious of it all of the time, I knew I carried it with me. It governed my relationships to my family and the time spent with loved ones. There was the fear of loss and, perhaps most significantly, the fear that I was somehow defective. Fear that I had somehow attracted this variety of suffering to me, like a rabbit who, stricken with trepidation, stands up in a field and shrieks its rabbit cry into the air, thereby announcing to the world and to every conceivable predator not only its location but its utter vulnerability. It was the fear that I was genetically predisposed somehow to loss and in its wake, precariousness of the mind's balance on the proverbial ledges it finds itself.

It occurred to me that it was perhaps the same hole in the sky through which my grandfather, years before my birth, had disappeared that Adrian and now seemingly all traces of the divine had flown. Perhaps I too threatened to depart through this threshold by which Violet's soul, too, had fled. She had left behind only the shell of her aging body to entertain us, offer us Shasta colas when we came to her small, stifling house for our thirty-five minute visits. Perhaps the rest of her, the effulgent lightness that is spirit and not flesh, had learned to vacate the body and ride the ether to her beloved, if not in waking hours, in her sleep. Of course even this intimacy with Grandpa Charlie, this tear in the fabric of her consciousness as evidence of how it broke her to lose him, was my invention, too. And was it better to be thought mad, promiscuous, negligent, while the mind traveled its fractured passages? Had she simply given up one way of being (in the world) for another (in her mind)? And where did that leave me? I who sought to live inside of a poem if it could be done.

It frightened me to think of this. To bring the similarities between my grandmother and myself into focus. I knew my friends thought it strange that I should go walking every night alone, that I should grow silent and dim, sequester myself in my apartment, emerging only to attend classes and not interacting with a single soul. "Much madness is divinest sense/ To a discerning eye," I would tell myself, but I had no way to assert my discernment over that of others who worried for me. My parents, old friends, even Adrian's mother.

I was not so self-indulgent as to compare my experience of loss to Violet's directly. I had not married Adrian and if I was honest with myself, I probably never would have. But it is the question of an uncertain future, one dictated by untimely death, a door closed to a tentative knock, that torments. I could not tolerate the introduction of events that I had not chosen but which had altered (or had appeared to alter) my course irrevocably. It was the Absurd, the seeming arbitrariness of suffering, doled out before me to Adrian's family and friends, to my grandmother and even to me, that frightened me so much.

No, my suffering did not even approach that of Violet. I had not borne three children and then been left with them, unskilled and with no visible means to support them, let alone myself. And yet the hollowness I had always seen in Violet's face, the black granite eyes we shared, was hauntingly familiar now, and I felt that I understood where it was she had receded to all these years.

I thought I understood what a disruption our family's visits must have been to the careful cultivation of mourning. Mourning that had lasted a lifetime and which added up, ultimately, to slow death. For after that moment on the porch, after the telegram that changed her course irrevocably, what was there for her to do but begin to die? Inadequate as she was for the task of healing, of accepting, and of sheltering her children from her grief, she succumbed to it wholly. She had allowed herself to spill away from them into the ether, chasing a ghost she might never find, for there was still no confirmation, decades later, that he was dead. No body to mourn, no bones to lay to rest on American soil.

She *should* have collected herself. Should have pulled it together for her sons who deserved a mother, if a sad one. She should have recovered over time and "moved on." So simple for a stranger to say. So stark a truth for my great uncles, who judged and discarded the woman their brother had loved in his living. I spent hours with this idea of Violet, too weak to move from her place of despair. And what determines that really? The sureness or the fragility of the soul? Is it a single gene that one might inherit? For here, in my own despair, grief had become comfortable, enchanting even. I spent my nights with it and let it govern my dreams. Was I like her? Had I inherited her weakness? These questions slipped around the interior of my soul during those restless, melancholy years. It would be so easy to check out, I thought. So easy to slip beneath a chenille bedspread and sleep until it was all over.

I began to dream of her, and sometimes in that dream space, I *was* her. Our shared self was hauntingly familiar but unique, no face I had ever known. At least not one I remembered. I would speak to myself *as* her, invent the conversations we might have if we could just bring ourselves out of that dream firmament and plant ourselves on the earth. She was invariably more powerful, more insistent than I, and where I would have dived down, dredged the bottom of a murky rock quarry, she would carry us upward, into a sky that was blue and limitless, searching, searching for a seam. I would wake feeling dizzy and disoriented, afraid that my brain was somehow slipping from my skull, from what was recognizably real.

When my feet touched the floor, when I had taken a shower and washed my hair and had drunk a cup of coffee or two, I would feel somewhat recovered, but it was like it took those activities, their mundanity and their realness, to bring me back to earth again. To the place I inhabited with the rest of the people in the world. It was an attractive milieu, though, that dream space. Comfortable. I would sometimes catch glimpses of Adrian there, suspended against that blue sky. He had grown to mythical proportions in my mind and finally, I came to understand, represented everything I had lost in that quarry: my innocence, my intrepidity, my utter faith. He was elusive and never came near, flitting away into my periphery each time I turned toward him. Still, it was a space in which I felt he might exist at least, and for that I clung to it. There he might occasionally brush up against me, whereas in my waking time, as I walked from season to season nursing something that I could not let go, he was far from me. A memory that was beginning to lose its vibrancy, beginning to lose its edges and thus its clarity.

Two years after my grandfather was declared Killed in Action, his own mother, my Great Grandmother Virgilia, climbed into her claw-foot tub dressed in her Sunday best--a lavender dress with fluttery chiffon sleeves (again, I invent in the absence of details). She gripped its porcelain bottom with bare toes and turned to face white tiles. She had clipped her fingernails to the skin, painted her thin lips a matte red and whispered, *I change it now.* As much air as voice.

She had chosen her husband's birthday for her departure (had she hated him that much?), and she had pulled her long black hair into a thick braid, moved it behind her thin shoulder and out of the way. With her hands she prepared the blade of a kitchen knife, ran it across flesh: pale underbelly of faith gone awry. MIA means *wait and please*, but her son was a shade among trees, and she knew. She knew he was not coming back to her, her favorite boy. Her baby. She had the same sense that Violet had of his absence, the minute it was suggested, though they never spoke of it, these two women from whom my own life had issued.

These were the two women whose lunacy gnawed at the edges of my own want then. My own sense of the godless vacuum into which we are born grew, until it encompassed all three of us and threatened to swallow me whole. In moments of clarity, I wanted to know: do we carry the suffering of our ancestors at a cellular level? Is it possible to escape the cycles of grief that seem to arrive like waves from far out at sea, insistent and without a perceptible end? And more importantly, do we inherit the madness of our mothers, our fathers?

When I looked in the mirror, I sometimes saw Violet. Not as she was when I visited her with my dad, but how I grew her in my imagination, though even in her dim living room at sixty-seven she showed me a reflection of myself: high cheekbones, angular chin, eyes abysmal in their darkness. Skin browner than our "Irish" heritage would allow. Of course Grandma Esther never gave me reason to believe that she was the woman I had fleshed out in my imagination, but I had no doubt. It was she, as Violet, who moved through my dream space like she owned it, me clinging to her like a wraith. How was she able to occupy the same space as Adrian? I resented her for it, and yet here, in the realm of the real, I craved her attention, her conversation, as if she held some key to my chamber of dreams. Whether she had a sense of my desire or not, she withheld it.

I remember arriving at her house one summer, carrying the customary birthday gift under one arm: a matching lounge set. This year it was pink and soft, a plush kind of fabric. The pants had a drawstring, and the top a tiny bow at the neckline. It seemed the thing to give her, my mother always said and, "I think she likes pretty things, too." My mother had pushed me out the door of the car with the gift-wrapped box. Once again my father and I would visit Grandma Esther alone while my mom and brother ran some half-hour errand. This time, I thought, I would gently, gently introduce a few questions about Grandpa Charlie, and I would share my own experience of grief with her.

I spoke in hushed tones, started from the beginning. Then I waited. If Grandma Esther had any emotional response to what I told her, of a bright and beautiful boy swallowed by root beer colored water in a rock quarry, of a girl bewildered by the incongruity of such a reality with her childhood faith, her countenance did not betray it. The baseball game moved distortedly in the lenses of her eyeglasses, and the TV cast a blue light on her face. She sat very still, her chin pushed forward in an almost pout. Finally, she made a sort of assenting sound in her throat that sounded more like humming than a response to my words.

I tried again: "Grandma, what was Grandpa Charlie like?" I asked her softly. Gently. Her eyes flicked from the television screen to the clock and back again, almost imperceptibly, and she made the same noise in her throat. That was all. I looked at my dad, who simply shrugged and looked resignedly out the window. It had taken me most of our visit to work myself up to this question, and my mother would be there soon. Deflated, I was silent for the next five minutes, only half conscious of the small talk that ensued: the prowess of the Toronto Blue Jays this year, rioting due to the acquittal of the white police officers who had beaten Rodney King, the closure of a local drugstore in Turlock. When our SUV pulled into the driveway and we got up to go, I hugged Grandma Esther, as I always did when we were leaving. With her mouth close to my ear, she let go a quiet but distinctly forceful sibilance: "Shhh." It was not unkind, but it was definitive. *Be quiet, child*, it said, and *Stop.* I did.

She faded into old age and into the yellowed walls
of her house, covered them with contact paper, hung
scissors, magazine cut-outs, key chains, paper dolls
from red and yellow thumbtacks. Her life, strung

across this background, layers of smoky residue, her heart
fell silent: in time it is only a matter of time
before MIA becomes less than a promise, and the art
of mourning swallowed her in its beauty. In time

her knotted jaws were set against news, against hope. Numb,
she let it all go. The three men after. Her children. The four
who left. And at what point had she succumbed
to the blue light of the TV? A woman's life is lost well before

her death. Wed now to the ivy that creeps across her siding,
pale green, in her slippered feet she talks and laughs of nothing.

Ironically, as if in response to my own questions, Virgilia's daughter Dolores, my Grandpa Charlie's sister, would continue the cycle set in motion by her mother, but decades later when she herself had become an old woman. Long after it seemed that the ash had stopped falling on the Carroll family, when it seemed all the mysteries had been sealed, Dolores, whose name in Spanish means "pains," would shoot herself in the stomach on *her* husband's birthday. Is it possible to love suffering so much?

Something would impel Dolores Carroll to repeat her mother's inconceivable act of suicidal defiance and do it in such a way as to protract the act of dying. Perhaps she had wanted, in all the years following her brother's disappearance, to know what it felt like to die. Perhaps her mother's choice had only piqued her curiosity and excited a kind of jealousy in her; why did her mother get to experience it and not she? What was the passage like, crossing from this life to the next? Even if the next was nothing but silence beneath cold earth, it would grow in her mind toward mythical splendor, so that finally, she could not resist its attraction.

I imagine her gravitation toward the unthinkable. Cold metal in her hand. Thumb on a trigger. Then this: Dolores lying on the bedroom floor, watching the crimson circle of her own blood expand around her softly trembling body, spilling from the flower of her blooming belly, the last warm thing. I imagine the morbid pleasure she must have felt in knowing that finally, finally, it was done and there was nothing left to agonize over.

I tell myself it is my imagination that allows me to adorn the act with such detail, not the relatability of the feeling that inspired it.

Chapter Five

April 1958, Bradford, Arkansas

Violet eventually took a job in the Bradford Public Library to try to make ends meet. A single mother of five now, my father and his brothers and the twins born to her with Dennis, Violet felt isolated from the rest of the world otherwise. Plus, the library gave her several quiet hours among the stacks, as well as hushed interactions with a number of people she would otherwise never encounter in a day. She wore horn-rimmed reading glasses, attached to her neck by a beaded cord, and sometimes low heels, a calico dress. Her beauty, faded though it was, was still enough to attract the odd reader or researcher, who would make any pretense to talk to the pretty librarian with graceful hands and a question in her eyes.

The Carroll boys were "tumbling up" in the Dickensian sense, only they were wholly independent and knew themselves as such. By now Ricky was ten, Matty eight and Baby Seb six, and during the week, while they were at school, the twins, now two years old and into everything, stayed with their Auntie Ruth. Ruthanne was Dennis's older half-sister, a spinster and a town fixture in Bradford, living off her father's money, modest as it was. Until the birth of the twins, Ruthanne Blake had spent all her time with her aviary of lovebirds.

Never having married or expressed the desire to do so, Ruthanne surprised the townsfolk by taking a lively interest in little Joseph and Edie, the nephew and niece who were perhaps the only gift her errant brother had ever given her. She was, it seemed, the only one interested in the children, with the occasional exception of Violet who would sometimes stop what she was doing, washing dishes or hanging laundry, and look at them with a surprised expression. Her eyebrows appeared as two capsized parentheses, drawn in brown pencil. It was as if she wondered for a moment where they had come from, what part of her life had yielded them, though Edie was already the spitting image of herself. Edie's black tuft of hair already resembled the raven feathers of her mother's now damaged tresses, the way they had been when my Grandpa Charlie had walked the earth and loved her. After such pauses, Violet would return to the task at hand, singing Patti Page songs in the velvety voice that had enchanted my grandfather and was perhaps the only evidence of the joy she had shared with him.

"Another time, another place, we'll be together again," she would croon, and who could tell what went on in her head as she intoned the words of a lost love. There could as easily have been nothing going on as everything. Ricky decided it was the former, and he would carry that disappointment with him, grow hard and become a pilot himself, follow his father with his life.

The Carroll boys, as they began to be known in town, were always a little bit dusty, a little unkempt, but they had their daddy's infectious smile, and people in town could not help but take to them. They were surprisingly well mannered, probably a residual effect of spending summers with Uncle Lawrence and Aunt Bernice in Conway, where life was different; chores were doled out and balanced with play time, whereas play time had to be scrapped for in their mother's realm. Chores did not exist in Violet's house either, as it were, but rather a kind of clean up detail that consisted of watching Violet and finishing whatever task she failed to complete. She seemed to move from room to room like a graceful ghost. Though she would bestow coveted smiles upon her boys at intervals, even touch them on the head or the cheek now and then, she was unavailable to them, and they knew.

Violet's black eyes revealed nothing of tenderness or recognition, though they shimmered in their glossy darkness and could still catch the attention of most men. Only Baby Seb had the courage to occasionally sneak into her room at night and lay his body alongside her warm figure there in the bed. He would listen to her breath, barely breathing himself, watching the rise and fall of her back, always turned to him. He would throw his suntanned arm over her body, clad in the slippery fabric of a full-length slip or, if she had thought to change, a cotton nightgown. It was a kind of remembrance of filial affection, a way of being that she had long forgotten and Baby Seb recalled only vaguely. There were so many things that Violet seemed not to recall.

Violet would hang the laundry, but Ricky would have to run out and rescue it from a rain shower days later. By then there would be holes in the long row of garments, the boys having dressed themselves each day from the line since it had dried. Violet would buy groceries but forget to put them away, so that if Ricky or Matty did not pass through the kitchen where the brown paper sacks had been left on the table, milk would spoil and cheese coagulate in its packaging. She spent more and more time with the books she brought home from the library in tall stacks. Books that must have held fabulous mysteries, Matty concluded, for they were more interesting to her than any conversation he might introduce, which after a while he stopped trying to do. Unexpectedly, however, she would sometimes bring a smaller stack and leave it on Matty's bed. They were books with fantastic stories that left him reeling, sent him into unseen realms of flight and fancy. They were her gift to him and perhaps the only acknowledgment of his inclination toward narrative and effectively crafted language, inherited of course from her. When he finished each book, he would place it on the corner of the coffee table, and it would disappear the next day when Violet left for work. When the stack was gone, there would be more, though sometimes after a gap of a day or a week, for Violet's attentions were inconsistent at best.

Over time they saw less and less of the twins, so that they seemed to be absorbed by Auntie Ruth and her house across town, simply expunged from their own lives without so much as a good bye. Violet had agreed weakly, in a private meeting with Ruthanne, that they might do better with a little more consistency, and she had waved her hand in acquiescence as Ruthanne had begun packing their tiny clothes and miniature shoes. She had enlisted Ricky and Matty to help her with this work, and they had exchanged concerned looks but did as they were told, until finally all traces of their half sister and brother were gone from the house, and the two of them had been packed into Ruthanne's Buick.

All three of the Carroll boys stood, somewhat forlorn, as the car pulled away from the yard. The twins were up on their knees in the sprawling back seat. Auntie Ruth's ornate bun, spun from her long grey hair, and her spidery hands atop the steering wheel at ten and two o'clock, were visible beyond them. Through the watery reflection of the birches in the yard, the boys could see the twins waving blankly out the back window until the car was out of sight. Edie's other hand was tucked under her nose, while she sucked her thumb, a habit that would surely give her buck teeth, Auntie

Ruth had opined, but Edie had been too young for an appeal to vanity to be effective.

There must have been tender moments, instances of raucous fun and laughter among the half siblings, but Matty and Ricky (and certainly Baby Seb) would forget them. They would keep only vague recollections of the pair, the sensation of pleasure in reading a book to little Edie or in bouncing little Joe on a knee for the "one-legged rodeo." There would always be a nebulous sense of loss, for Matty especially, but it was not tangible enough to address, and they were too young to give it much thought. Life is one way for a time, and then something changes, and it goes on another way. Such was their experience of it, in any case. It was a kind of forced non-attachment, I think, but it worked to save them from the hurt of it.

May 1959, Bradford, Arkansas

When Randall Pruitt showed up at the dinner table one night, where the boys were summoned to an uncustomary sit-down dinner, they were instantly suspicious of the slick, guitar-playing truck driver who brought a new quality to their mother's smile. It was not attraction exactly, but more of a benign resignation and perhaps a dim hope of relief from something only she knew was a threat. It was beautiful enough, that smile, together with her billowing hair, which was still not her raven black but had been brought back, with multiple dye jobs, to a hue closer to her natural color. Randall was greedy, it seemed, sucking the meat off the bones at dinner with a satisfied sound that disgusted Ricky and fascinated Baby Seb. And he looked at Violet greedily, too, liberally sending his hand across her shoulder or, to Matty's alarm, along her thigh.

When it was announced that they were moving to California with Randall in his Chevy pickup truck, the boys did not say a word, but Ricky and Matty immediately began conspiring to stay together in Bradford. Only after their scheming yielded no reasonable way for them to take care of themselves and their baby brother who, it was determined, could not be left with Violet and Randall alone, did they abandon their plan. They had even approached Auntie Ruth, riding the five and a half miles to her house along the canal on borrowed bikes, but she had pursed her lips and shaken her head firmly, a look of regret but also determination on her drawn face. Her lovebirds had been making a sweet little racket in the background, the boys would remember, and Auntie Ruth had not offered them a chance to say good bye to the twins, who were nowhere in sight.

The boys had taken to calling their mother by her first name in private conversations among themselves. It meant something that they could assert themselves in this way, but they did it without processing the symbolism of their small linguistic rebellion. They had become tough, clear-eyed little fellows, pragmatic in every way. At school they had friends and successes, both academic and athletic, but Ricky's performance was erratic. Without guidance from home he would gravitate away from education and toward a kind of intelligence that could be measured with his body. First on the ground and then in the air at the helm of a Huey helicopter. Matty derived more pleasure from the praise of his teachers and thrived on the approbation he received in that arena. Seb, still so young, simply clung to his brothers like a mud turtle but also, inexplicably, to his mother.

They were to have one last summer with Uncle Lawrence, who assured Violet that the boys would be delivered to her in California. Randall had a job waiting there and Violet could get one at the local cannery paying nearly twice as much as she had earned at the library. She quickly found that working at the cannery also required almost twice as much of her time as the library had and left her back and feet aching each night. It was not Violet's way to complain but rather to continue living, allowing others to steer her gently away from imminent dangers while she receded without fanfare further into her personal obscurity. She could be brought back at intervals, it seemed, but never for good.

I know that Uncle Lawrence looked into legally adopting my father and his brothers that summer, got all his ducks in a row, but Violet had refused, revealing some latent maternal streak that surprised everyone. Uncle Lawrence and Aunt Bernice had not counted on her waking from her walking slumber to refuse them, and though they consulted lawyers and did all the legwork necessary, in the end they had to accept that it just was not possible to take children from a mother who was not willing to release them. Emotional negligence is an invisible abuse, nearly impossible to prove, and when asked tensely and point blank by their mother on the phone, "Do you want to live with your Uncle Lawrence now? Is that it?" the boys gently conceded that they missed her and that no, they would like to come to her and Randall in California.

The drive out was sweltering-August-hot and grimly quiet, but something in my father was growing with each mile. Sitting with Baby Seb wedged between himself and Ricky on the bench seat of Uncle Lawrence's pickup, there was a sort of suppressed excitement in his nine-year-old heart. It had to do with change. Possibility. A new horizon beyond which any kind of life might be visible. He had already decided that he wanted to be a teacher like he knew his father had been, before he had enlisted, and California probably had lots of kids, he reasoned. Lots more than Bradford. And they'd all need educating. Funny how childhood dreams survive the crushing blows of adult failures. How no matter how much darkness envelopes them, there is always a little light, and they never fail to perceive it. Ricky was nearly twelve then and was on borrowed time with regard to that light, had already begun to let bitterness seep into his consciousness, but it would be some time before he would turn away from Violet in earnest. He would join the Army and unapologetically exit the way his father did, first to war and then to peaceful rest, head bowed to his chest in a tangled heap of helicopter debris in Vietnam.

Chapter Six

April 1994, San Luis Obispo, California

Four years after Adrian, almost to the day, I met Zach. I was not ready in any way to have a relationship, but Zach was sweet and patient and happy to spend time with me, whatever it meant. I met him at the San Luis Obispo farmers' market, where I worked at a little barbecue stand scooping pulled pork for foot traffic: people who knew that BDB meant "Best Damn Barbecue." This was the name of the little restaurant that, like all the other businesses on Higuera, took to the street every Thursday night the whole year 'round. My friend Kristina and I, who had both been sworn vegetarians for years, served barbecue sandwiches to college kids (our peers then) and to local families, as well as to myriad travelers who had heard of the quaintness and liveliness of the SLO weekly farmers' market. It was good money and easy work, and it put us smack in the center of the action every week, which is probably why Kristina suggested the gig to me. She had a tendency to mother me and though I resisted it, I let her.

Kristina was one of the few of my friends who had known Adrian and known me in the weeks where I was speaking at his memorial services, both in his hometown and in San Luis Obispo, and losing my self in layers, until finally I was a pathetic heap of disillusionment. She had been my roommate in the dormitory and had never left my side. She had lit candles and put her hand on my back, singing quiet hymns on the nights I could not stop weeping. She had listened to me tell stories of my love for Adrian and never reminded me that we had been on rocky ground before he died. Never scolded me for my romantic rendering of what had been imperfect at best. Her soft grey-green eyes were gentle, as was her voice, and there was a dogged tenacity to her love.

Kristina had taken me hiking, bicycling, boating. Anything to pull me out of my self-indulgent grief and make me breathe the air. "I wish you would look at the hay," Jane Kenyon had written years before, "the sane and solid beautiful bales of hay." It was a sweet little poem called "Evening at a Country Inn," and it has spoken to me in so many ways over the years. "You laughed only once all day--/ when the cat ate cucumbers in Chekhov's story," Kenyon had written. That was me; the only reprieve I ever found from the heaviness of living seemed to be in books, in the stories and poems of others. The speaker in Kenyon's poem urges the *you* she addresses to notice anything, *anything* but the trauma that keeps replaying itself in his mind.

Kristina wanted me to look at anything but the hole in my faith, the blackness left by Adrian's extraction and the detritus of a belief system shot to hell by events with which I could not reconcile myself. In the two years that followed his death, she continued to be my roommate, tolerating all manner of bizarre behavior and allowing me to keep a stray cat, even though she was severely allergic. She was that kind of friend.

This night at farmers' market, a tall boy with long brown curls bleached out by sun and enchantingly green eyes came through our barbecue line. His face was handsome in all the conventional ways, and I was inclined to ignore him, but something about his gaze arrested me. He smiled at my slight discomfiture, not out of arrogance but out of delight, for he was as taken with me standing there in a dirty white line cook apron and holding out to him a steaming pile of meat that secretly reviled me. His voice, I noticed when he thanked me, had in it the golden sand of beaches. A kind of soft, gravelly quality that belied ocean waves and an organic kind of music, always present just beneath the surface of sound.

Yes, I think it can be said that it was Zach's voice I fell in love with first, all two syllables I had heard of it. His voice had the ocean in it. I had stopped surfing when Adrian died, only one of the ways I had denied myself for the past few years. It felt strained and strange to do something so wholly non-industrious. Something whose only purpose was my own edification. Fun, as it were. I had unconsciously bound myself to the land, too, spent a great deal of time on it where the asphalt ended and the dusty soil of the Central Coast began. I was engaged most of the time in a kind of moving meditation where I coddled my grief by resisting most efforts to draw me out of it, and this was the business of earth. Not sea.

Zach's voice was a cool wave over my desiccated heart. Something about it reminded me of the weightlessness I had known in the water, of the benediction of a wave over my head as I duck dived, pushing my board beneath its rise and punching through to the other side. It had in it a promise, which is probably the only reason that when he handed me a piece of paper as he was being spirited away by a gaggle of other surfer boys at the end of the night, I did not throw it away with the rest of the debris from a night of the farmers' market melee. Instead I tucked it in my pocket and forgot about it until the next morning.

When I awoke the sun was already pouring itself into my room, sectioned by the thin, measured shadows of my mini-blinds. My young Tabby cat Sophia was stretching her body long in that segmented light, exulting in its warmth and the prospect of the first sunny day in a week. I need not have been surprised; the sky last night had been crystalline, each star a lucid pinpoint of white light appearing to escape what lay beyond the blue-black canvas of the night. I remember thinking as Kristina and I had walked home at evening's end that such a sky was auspicious and certainly meant fair weather for the upcoming weekend. We had giggled at ourselves, walking home with barbecue sauce under our fingernails and smoke in our hair. We were a mess, as always after the market, but something about the night felt good…to both of us.

In the morning, my pillow was still damp from having gone to bed with a wet head; I peeled several strands of damp hair from my cheek and reached over to my jeans, which lay on the floor exactly where I had stepped out of them. I felt in the back pocket for the boy's note and pulled it out. In angular, forward slanted handwriting, the following:

I caught the happy virus last night
When I was out singing beneath the stars.
It is remarkably contagious--
So kiss me.

--Hafiz

A boy who does not deign to flatter and refrains from begging for a phone number. Instead he gives a Persian poem and asks for nothing…except a kiss that has no means to find its way to him. I was interested, for sure, but it was clear that he was visiting from out of town and that most likely I would never see him again. I did not even know his name. Still…

Like that, a little dream of love was ignited: tiny flame of belief that had seemed long ago extinguished. Belief in connection between two humans who might be generous toward one another, not greedy or grasping. Aparigraha: though it is often defined as "non-possessiveness," I had come to understand its meaning as *not grasping.* Not desperately trying to hold onto what naturally moves away from us like the tide. On some level I knew that this was my problem. If I could only embrace aparigraha, then perhaps the tense fear of loss might melt away from me. The way I approached every moment as a possible finality. The way I considered, with every departure from friends and family, how the good byes we exchanged measured up, in case they were the last ones. This way of living, anticipating loss and even death, made for a strained existence at best.

I recognized that aparigraha was something that might allow me to breathe, remove the corset of fear that circumscribed every act, every interaction with others, if only it could be achieved. It was one of the Yamas, or codes of self-restraint, which I had begun to study in my shift away from the more vigorous activities of running and surfing and toward the science of surrender through yoga. I would stand, bathed in the morning light streaming through the French doors of my living room, and face the sun, salute it again and again, reminding myself of its vigor, of my own life force, of the goodness in my flagging self, lest I forget and somehow let it slip away.

I had grown thin and slight, less hardy and less vital. I was amazed at how quickly muscle melts away from the body when it is neglected. I took up less and less space in the world. Soon, I remember having thought, perhaps I would disappear all together. I was looking for ways to repose, relax into my existence and accept my life path, which seemed to sprawl tiresomely and interminably before me. I simply had less energy for dynamic movement and physical power. I wanted to be still. At least this is how I explained it to Kristina, but she, in her mother hen role, worried that I was giving up. That like Violet, I had begun to slowly die. Unlike Violet, though, I would do it well and with consciousness, I thought, though I did not speak this aloud. Kristina would have probably staged an intervention if I ever lent any credence to her theories of my slow departure.

And now, here was a boy. Or here he was not, for how might I ever find him to deliver a word, let alone that kiss? I Scotch-taped the little handwritten note with Hafiz's poem inside my journal and kept moving. Day to day, class to class, poem to poem. Breath to breath.

I had one year left of graduate work. Having entered an MFA program in writing, I had relished the appeal of moving more and more into the realm of language, lifting up and away from real life, which was much less satisfying, much less alive for me. Emily Dickinson said in a letter to a friend that just the "essence of living" was enough to bring her joy, and I felt a certain affinity for the woman who had lived her adult life almost exclusively in her room, swimming in the poems that would later grace the Harvard library and be mass published, but which in her lifetime simply provided the lyrical sea to her fish-like self.

Something moved in me, though, when I heard Zach's voice. *Thank you*, he had said, and he was of course referring to the sandwich in my hand, but something in his voice sang to me. Two words in reference to pork and somehow they choreographed the primitive first steps of my salvation. They sang of a distant feeling I'd had, years ago, on the sea. *On the sea.*

That day after I met Zach, the day I had read his intrepid little note containing Hafiz's poem, I drove out to Los Osos for the first time in three years. I drove beyond the sand dunes and parked my pickup, began the brief and winding hike through towering Eucalyptus trees to my favorite break there called Hazards. A handful of other cars was there, too, so I knew there would be waves, and I walked through the wooded area, slipping in my sneakers on the slightly muddy trail, a hint of the old anticipation rising in my ribcage. As I went, I removed layers of clothing, first a hoodie, then a thermal, until finally I wore a thin camisole that, once the path opened onto the rocky shore, exposed my arms, shoulders and neck to a brilliant sun and the cool spring air.

I watched the surfers scan the horizon for lines that would lift upward as they approached, the water dragging itself over underwater terrain and then cresting and peeling across the little bay. A slight offshore breeze sent a fine spray of water over the backs of the waves and added a steepness, a quickness to their breaking. An exuberant little hoot broke the air as a surfer kicked out of a sweet little four-footer, and shielding my eyes to the sun, I could see that his board shorts dragged behind him, looped onto his leash, his bare ass glistening in the mid-day light. The "hoot" must have been as much from the cold as from sheer enjoyment. He flipped his long hair over his head and began his paddle back out into the freezing lineup. I could see then, once I began to focus, that there were three others who had doffed their boardies to "surf naked." They, too, were relishing in the glassy waves and the liberation from their wetsuits, which, I noticed then, were lined up like four black seals on the rocks just out of reach of the tide.

I walked tentatively to the water's edge. Hazards is not a nice, sandy beach but a rocky, rugged coastline, and the water in spring is about 56 degrees. I kicked my shoes back toward the shore as I made my way, fully clothed, into the water, catching my breath as it reached my thighs, my midriff, my shoulders. Under I went. I gave a little hoot myself on emerging from the icy water, but I felt good. Something in me had broken loose, and I dove under a little inside wave that reached me where I stood, balanced precariously on underwater stones. Once under it, beyond it, I was swimming. Floating and swimming and bobbing in the sea: unexpected baptism, release not sought.

I stayed there, floating on my back for some time, blinded by the yellow sun overhead, listening to the inner workings of the ocean and letting one foot, then the other, float down toward the ocean floor, my blue jeans heavy with their drink. My skin became taut, goose bumped in the freezing cold, tingling with the life of the sea. When I finally lifted my head and made my way to the shore, the naked boys had gone and their seal-like wetsuits with them. I was alone and filled with the sensation that had all but died in me, or so I had thought. It was, undeniably, faith…in myself and yes, in the divine. No wonder I had not been able to detect it. For me, divinity resided in the sea. It was an easy enough epiphany. *I must make my way back to it. Must immerse myself again*, I told myself, and it was the simplest of truths.

Several weeks passed before I saw Zach again. It turned out he had a friend who had gone to school in San Luis Obispo and who had many ties to the area. Zach made sure to be on the next SLO excursion in hopes, he later admitted to me, of seeing the sad and beautiful girl at the barbecue stand once more. I blanched at the description, not only because I did not consider myself 'beautiful,' but also because I was unaware of my emotional transparency, even to this stranger. But Zach was gentle and it was not his intention to judge. What was perhaps most refreshing about Zach was his artlessness. He was, above all, real. He was grounded and faithful to what he observed as true. He was frank and seemed not to fear judgment, perhaps because he himself always reserved it. How could he presume to judge another? It was *all good*, as he was fond of saying, and the more time I spent with him, the more I could see that this might be true.

By the end of June, Zach was coming up to SLO nearly every weekend, but that did not change the fact that he had a one-way ticket to Hawaii, which he had purchased before we ever met, and his departure date was fast approaching. Just in time to catch the winter swells. As a freelance photographer he had the freedom to roam, capturing images that would pay the bills as he went. He had gotten his foot in the door at *Extreme Sportsman Magazine* during an internship the previous year, and there were already murmurs of bringing him on staff full time, but for now Zach preferred to work for himself, with all the uncertainty and scrapping that such an existence entailed. He had made enough contacts during his time with the magazine, particularly an array of writers who had a predilection for the stark realism of his photography, his gift for capturing natural light, that he got enough gigs to support his Spartan lifestyle…and his penchant for surfing.

Zach had coaxed me back onto a surfboard after only a couple of weeks of spending time together, had been surprised by my proclivity for surfing big waves. We quickly fell into a pattern of paddling out together at dawn, letting the sunlight spill over our bodies as it rose over the Eucalyptus grove behind us. We would often have an hour alone together on the water before any other surfer made his way into the lineup, and we would sit in comfortable silence between waves, or we would speak softly, reverently, of things that mattered to us. It was a golden time, the first peacefulness I had known in three years, and I knew it as fleeting, anticipated its end with no small amount of apprehension. As with all pleasures in my life, I lived those days with fear lurking just over my shoulder, sometimes allowing it to settle into the space between my shoulder and my ear. In those times I would become reticent and withdraw into my journals or my books. Somehow, miraculously, when I did this, Zach would wait. Without complaint or inquiry, he would wait for me to come back to him, to close the distance I had reeled out between us with my own hand.

The next weekend would come, or the next northward road trip, that would land Zach at my door and, the fear having lifted, I would fall into him again. No questions. No conditions. After a surf session we would make our way into SLO-town and our favorite bake shop, or we would skip straight to the serious stuff and hit up Taqueria Vallarta. My appetite slowly began to return to me, and I grew stronger. The ocean in Zach's voice had called me back to the sea, to my aquatic self. The ocean of language, I found, was awfully dry without the counterbalance of time spent in the saltwater of Morro Bay or Los Osos National Park. We would sometimes head south, too. To Pismo Beach, which locals had dubbed "Dismo," because of its gray skies and inconsistent offering of waves. Even those days were alive with the light of our new friendship. My new way of being.

Still, I was ever aware of Zach's approaching travel date. Our friendship had bloomed into something very real. Very satisfying. And yet I had no intention of following him to Hawaii. It would not be *following* him, he said, quibbling with the semantics of the thing, but we both knew my reluctance had nothing to do with pride or feminism or any other sentiment that might cause me to object to the phrasing. I had made it clear from the beginning that I was not ready, that I was not looking for a commitment of any kind. Zach had acquiesced to this, but he had proposed that we spend as much time together as we could, seeing as it was so enjoyable for both of us, and I could not deny that it was. It was summer, after all, and we had so much fun together, even if it was only to sit and talk over Woodstock's pizza and root beer, so late into the night that the sky lightened with dawn; and he had of course led me back to the sea, for which I would be eternally grateful. But this. *Hawaii*? No.

When he left it was hard. I will not deny that now, and I did not deny it then. He was the most luminous person I had ever known. He had patience for every single one of my eccentricities, which ranged from bizarre food rules (fruit ONLY in its natural state, for example--no smoothies, no pies, no jam) to the neurotic insistence of sitting always to his left, regardless of location and irrespective of inconveniences it might incur. He liked it that laughter was my stress response, making me nearly unreadable in tense situations, and he thought it was funny that I found and eschewed grammatical errors in everything from news broadcasts to roadway billboards. He liked to hold my hand but did so only in private, always respectful of my guarded autonomy. He liked the smell of my hair and the smoothness of my skin, which he proclaimed particularly fine across my belly.

Zach was an artist through and through, and he was beautiful. Truly beautiful. In fact, it was fairly ridiculous how good-looking he was. I was constantly aware, though not jealous, for his unequivocal preference for my company nullified such a sentiment, of the constant attention he received from females of all ages. Either he ignored them or he was truly unaware of them, but he never wavered in his attention toward me. Too good to be true, really, was what I reasoned, and I kissed him good bye that October afternoon, knowing that things between us would forever be changed by my choice, not only to stay behind but also to refuse his offer to stay. No, I had said, he had this planned. It was his heart's desire. If we were to be together, it would happen, without us having to "rough hew" the destinies we had already set in motion. And he went alone, albeit reluctantly, to Lahaina. With only two surfboards in board bags and one oversized duffel, he boarded a plane to the wave-riding, art-creating, sun-kissed life he had laid out for himself before he ever met me.

Chapter Seven

January 1966, Turlock, California

In January of 1966, Matty left home for good. He was a month shy of sixteen and though he regretted leaving Baby, who was now fourteen and called Seb by everyone but his own family, Matty felt he had no choice. Ricky had left only a month earlier, not even waiting until Christmas to gather his things and enlist as a pilot in training, his sights set on Vietnam. It seemed that the months between September and December were to forever embody tumult for the Carroll family, though of course Violet was on the fourth last name of her life and as removed from the rest of the Carroll clan as she could be. Only her Baby Sebastian, named for the patron saint of soldiers, remained. He would stay until his eighteenth birthday and, having dutifully served his obligatory sentence, he would leave too.

When Randall Pruitt came home after a four-day bender and in broad daylight shot a clean hole through the living room window of their Turlock farmhouse with a .22 shotgun, Matty had had enough. He tried not to look at Baby's bewildered face, his angular shoulders quivering with uneven breath as he watched his older brother pack his things into a brown paper sack. Matty valued very little of what he kept here: some clothes, an extra pair of shoes. A worn copy of *Gulliver's Travels* that he had stolen from the Bradford Public Library that summer they left Arkansas for good.

He put a black Goody comb into his back pocket and handed Baby his leather jacket. It was a bomber jacket he had picked up at the Salvation Army shop in Ceres with money he had earned mowing lawns. Baby had envied his find ever since he had bought it, and now he held it in his hands, stroking the distressed leather and watching Matty with his dark eyes.

Baby knew he was lucky to have had his brothers this long. He, too, would leave his mother's house in time, but not yet. She needed him maybe. Who was going to protect her from Randall, after all, if he got mean again? Matty donned his shearling-lined corduroy coat, a grown-up sized near replica of the one he had worn as a toddler, stuffed the paper bag under one arm and pulled a package of cigarettes from inside his bureau. He gave Baby a brusque, one-armed hug that smashed his face against the brown corduroy of his coat and then left without looking back into the room where Baby still sat on the edge of the bed. He had begun to cry softly.

That was the last time he saw his mother for quite a while, for Matty refused to return to Violet's house until Randall left it. She was pregnant with Randall's second baby and still nursing his first, so he knew it would be no time soon, and so did Seb. He could hear the infant Violet had named Amelia wailing and his mother and Randall fighting as he made his way down the road in the January sunlight. Their voices had melded into a general disturbance by the time he reached the end of the almond orchard and finally, when he reached the canal, they had been silenced by the distance his sneakers had put between them.

He was headed to a friend's house, my "Uncle Jed's," where he would be coddled by Jed Kendall's five sisters in their Pentecostal home across town. He would be allowed to live out his high school days under their family's roof. The only payment required was three hours of his time every Sunday at their Pentecostal church services, where he would watch wide-eyed the hosts of people clapping and dancing in the aisles, visited by the Holy Ghost and inspired to do things like speak in tongues. It was well worth the hot meals, the clean rooms and fresh linens that appeared on a bed of his own every week. And the feminine attention of five doting women, who would occasionally let their luxurious locks slip from beneath their head coverings and whose infectious laughter filled the house with its music daily, was enough to make any boy a happy one.

And Jed was his best friend. Together they got into every manner of mischief and attracted every female from Turlock to Oakdale without batting an eye. They played together on the Turlock High football team, but they maintained their "greaser" status with weekend antics that would have made their Pentecostal "sisters" weak in the knees. The girls knew the boys got into trouble and were "naughty" sometimes, but perhaps their blissful ignorance was a grace to all of them. After a night of raucous behavior, parking lot fights and Thunderbird consumption, the boys would wake on a Saturday morning to banana pancakes and sizzling bacon, hot coffee and the five fresh-faced smiles of Jed's sisters. Their clean laundry would often be folded at the foot of their beds and their dirty clothes from the night before already whisked away into the next load.

Life was good for my dad, now called Matthew, for the two and a half years that he spent in the Kendall household. He would hear from Ricky occasionally from his training post and later from Vietnam by mail, and he would run into Baby at school. He pushed Violet and her coldness far away from his mind and into the obscurity where there dwelt all of the darknesses of his previous lifetimes, for so they felt to him: Bradford, Arkansas in the warm circle of his parents' love; Bradford in the shadow of his father's absence; Bradford with (and without) his twin half-siblings abandoned by Dennis Blake; the violence of Turlock with Randall Pruitt and Violet, pregnant twice more. All of these incarnations seemed to him a series of unsettling dreams that had left him here, in the home of the Kendall family. He was feeling his oats right now, sure, but he had never forgotten his plan to follow his father in education, and he knew he would straighten out just as soon as he had a mind to.

June 1967, Turlock, California

Ricky was not in Vietnam for six months when his helicopter was shot down just south of Quang Ngai on a rescue mission. The crash into leaning coconut trees bordering golden sand, something you might see on a post card except for the smoke, killed him and his three passengers almost instantly. One, a severely bleeding soldier from Kansas, was just eighteen years old and would probably not have lived anyway. The other two were fathers of small children, husbands of waiting women, from states on opposite coasts of the United States.

Ricky had been struck by the arbitrariness of such a confluence of lives that would end together on Vietnamese soil. This was his last thought before his Huey spun wildly out of the sky and into the curving trunks of a stand of palms. The trees edged the Sa Huynh Beach and were backed by rice paddies, where in another time Vietnamese men and women farmed and fished and launched their small boats. Perhaps it was a providence that Ricky and his cohorts would be spared participating in the massacre of Vietnamese villagers only about seventy kilometers to the north at Son My, which would occur nearly one year later and haunt the men involved for the rest of their living days. Small mercies.

Ricky's death came as no surprise to Violet, who was still married to Randall Pruitt, less violent now and more loving in his drunkenness, and who now had two little girls at home. Violet's life with her three sons, the children of her Charlie, now seemed more distant to her than the Southeast Asian coast upon which her eldest had perished. She and Randall attended services arranged and paid for by Uncle Lawrence and Aunt Bernice in Arkansas and did not object to burying Ricky next to his father's bodiless grave in the Oak Grove Cemetery in Conway. A bronze star adorned his headstone, just like his father's, though there was certainty interred beneath his, while his father's star spangled stone was ornamental, suggested a likely demise but insisted on nothing, the coffin beneath it apologetically empty.

It was here over the open grave of his brother that Matthew encountered his mother for the first time in the year and a half since he had left home. Randall chose not to acknowledge the young man, now seventeen years old, the captain of his high school football team, going into his senior year and resembling a twentieth century Adonis. His sinewy arms strained under the weight of his brother's rosewood coffin, carried with three other boys, including his younger brother Sebastian. They moved from the shiny black hearse to green manicured lawn, the shiny casket wedged in the space between shoulders and jaws, balanced by strong hands, serious faces.

At the grave's edge, Violet looked at Matthew for a moment as if stunned, so great was the likeness to Charlie, the man whose disappearance had vaguely directed all of the chaotic strands of her later life. When Matthew turned toward her, Violet lifted her hand, as if to touch his face. He closed his eyes to receive it, loosely aware of what touch could do to heal a distance, but when nothing followed he opened them again.

Violet had already turned back to face the minister who was preparing to speak. She had already abdicated the opportunity to touch her son, as she was in the habit of doing. Matthew endured the day without weeping, his jaw set firmly against it. Violet and Randall climbed into their blue Chevy Impala immediately following the ceremony and headed back to California, while Mathew and Seb, along with Uncle Lawrence, mingled with family and friends, most of whom were strangers to the two brothers, over Aunt Bernice's meatloaf and roast potatoes.

As the sun set on that day, its orange light blazing over Matthew's skin where he stood on Uncle Lawrence's front porch, he felt something settle in his guts. Felt a kind of resolve enter his consciousness, almost like his skeleton was hardening into its permanent shape inside of him. His brother was gone. The boy by whom he had set his compass in his earlier years no longer walked the earth but had fled his mortal body. Like his father before him.

His mother was still inadequate, it seemed, for the job of mothering, though she continued to procreate, as if perhaps by some providence she might grow into the role. Might become what was so natural a thing to be for so many other women he had observed. How could she not be what it was in her to be? What was so definitively missing from her composition that she seemed incapable of loving, let alone nurturing? It was a question that rose in his heart but which he chose not to attempt to answer. Some part of him pitied his own mother, he realized, and as the last pinpoint of red light bent over the fields spanning away from Conway, he leaned over the banister and vomited without making a sound.

It was during that trip out to Conway, protracted for the summer so that Matthew and Seb could spend one last season with their aunt and uncle and work haying on the neighbor's farm until school started in the fall, that my father determined to return the following year to Conway. He would attend the State College of Arkansas where his father Charlie Carroll had gone in the years it was called the Arkansas State Teachers College. He would complete two years of study in English Literature before he would move back to Turlock to attend Stanislaus State University and marry my mother, but that would come later. For now he worked tirelessly at baling golden hay from sunrise until sunset, wearying the body in a way that satisfied his grief and occupied his mind, stilling its proclivity for the philosophical questioning he was not yet willing to indulge.

Chapter Eight

February 1995, San Luis Obispo, California

After Adrian died, after I saw his mother lose her only son, I vowed never to have children. The anachronism of a mother seeing her child die was incomprehensible to me, a violation of nature and of the divine, which I forsook for a long time thereafter. The prospect of living for sixty more years or so seemed like a jail sentence to me then, and I remember feeling so weary, as though a long life were a curse. In the infinity of breathing that seemed to sprawl out before me, I did not intend to risk losing in the way I had watched Adrian's mother lose. Aching in the way I had seen her ache. I knew how to avoid it, and I set the intention to do so. It was not such an effort, after all, because out of habit I remained so closed to everyone that the cultivation of a mere friendship, let alone a romantic relationship of that caliber, was highly unlikely.

Even my parents, whose timid forays into my realm came in various tentative forms, could not penetrate the barrier of that distance. A sweet letter penned by my mother, a phone call to commemorate my cat's birthday, a surprise visit from the two of them and an Amtrak trip down to Santa Barbara for some "R & R, just the three of us"...these things provided a kind of lifeline that kept me from lifting off completely, disappearing into the stratosphere of my self-imposed alienation. But they could not bring me back to Earth. My parents felt at odds, I could see, but it was all I could do to yield to their generosities. I knew myself as far away from them, from every human contact, and perhaps unreachable (I could barely make them out from that height, small as they were against the variegated landscape of Earth, their hands above their eyes to shield them from the sun. Peering up. Straining to see me).

Then came along this boy with the ocean in his voice. Zach with salt drying along his temples, with the sunlight in his hair. With him it had been different. I had agreed easily to his little proposal of sharing as much time as we could together until his departure. Time spent with Zach was comfortable, simply *good.* I would ignore this fundamental difference in our relationship, the fact that I had allowed him to reel me in, set my feet down in the soil next to him, and then to move me toward the water. Toward my oceanic home. The element I had forsaken in my grief, in my searching. I would chalk it up to our commitment to non-commitment, or even to our awareness of the temporality of our experience together, bounded as it was by the Pacific Ocean and a one-way plane ticket. Perhaps it *was* the fact that we knew it was ending that we cherished it so much; in any case, I could think of a million reasons not to call it love.

Whatever it was, it made way for something extraordinary to occur. Something from which, had I seen it coming, I would probably have fled, so keen was my sense of self-preservation. The truth was, though, that by the time Zach left for Hawaii we had cultivated a profound love that was somehow more raw and real in the absence of the intention to do so. I had opened myself to him, impossibly it seemed, before I had even realized it was happening.

At the top of an enormous spiral staircase that rose above the ocean just south of San Luis Obispo, Zach had taken my left hand in both of his, had knelt on one knee and asked in earnest, "Meghann Carroll, will you be my best friend?" He had slipped a delicate silver ring with a small moonstone setting onto my index finger, encircled my hips with his arms, laying his head softly against my belly. After a few moments of silence, I sank into the nest of his body, fitting myself beneath his chin, and we remained there, letting the sea air move in us until it was dark and the gulls had quieted.

In the week before he left, I who had been so careful to preserve my Mary-like purity (I was the only twenty-two year old virgin I or any of my friends knew), gave myself in earnest to the boy I was sending away from me. We had climbed to the top of Cerro San Luis Obispo wearing woolen socks and fleeces against the encroaching fall chill, and we had found a little ravine that spilled out onto a small clearing of yellow grasses. With the whole of San Luis Obispo tumbling away from us in the dusky sunset light, our mountain nestled in among its eight sisters, we made love under a sunset sky.

Zach was so gentle, so full of sweetness and gratitude, and I knew without having any comparison at all, that he was the most generous of lovers. He was gentle with my body, moved in me with great care, cognizant all the time of what it was I offered to him that day. Perhaps it should not have surprised me then, having scrapped the first rule engendered in the loss of Adrian, when, two months after Zach had gone, I found that I was to violate the second: I was pregnant. *Hapai*, as they say in Hawaiian, full with the new life that had sprung from our love and my innocent gift.

For two months after this discovery I struggled with morning sickness, which is a complete misnomer, I found, as "morning" sickness occurs around the clock with no apparent preference for the early hours of the day. Mostly I just felt like I would vomit every moment. Sometimes I did. I also struggled with sharing the news of the pregnancy with Zach. I never intended to keep it from him as long as I did, and it never crossed my mind to keep it from him indefinitely, but I feared what it might do to our perfect intention. To the freedom from obligation of any sort, which we had inhabited all the time we were together.

I feared how vulnerable it had made me, first to love him and now to be carrying his child, but I was not foolish enough to believe that by resisting Zach's presence in my life I would be less so. It was done, and I was hopelessly, deeply connected to him. In my heart I returned to the concept of *Om*. Had we not always been connected in this way? Since before we met, perhaps even since before we were born? And was it not our acknowledgment, our permission, which could make that connection holy now? My body bloomed with motherhood, opening and swelling with the life we had created together, while my consciousness seemed to undergo a parallel expansion. I felt fiercely protective of all that we had grown together, especially this mysterious little life inside of me.

In the first weeks of Zach's absence, we had spoken on the phone every few days, and then, after the first phone bills started arriving, we deferred to the postal service for our correspondence. Neither Zach nor I possessed personal computers. Zach worked with film, of course, it being the 90's, and had no need of digital capabilities; I preferred my little word processor to the daunting expenditure a full-fledged computer would require and remained fairly disconnected from the world of the Internet. So we began to write letters, the content of which was always lively and varied on Zach's end, always poetic and somewhat melancholy on mine.

On a foggy morning in late February 1994, after an ultrasound appointment that revealed that I was carrying a daughter, I scribbled this excerpt from a Rumi poem on a small scrap of paper and mailed it to Zach on Maui:

This being human is a guest house.
Every morning a new arrival.
A joy, a depression, a meanness,
some momentary awareness comes as an unexpected visitor.
Welcome and entertain them all!
Even if they're a crowd of sorrows,
who violently sweep your house
empty of its furniture,
still, treat each guest honorably.
He may be clearing you out
for some new delight.

--Rumi

Zach knew immediately what it meant. Without calling me he booked a flight in to Santa Barbara and drove up in a friend's car. He showed up at my door, breathless and flushed from the cold. When I opened the door it was as if I was absorbed by him. He took me in his arms and breathed into my hair, my neck, and then my hands as he backed me up so that he could observe my new shape. It was not so different from what it had been before, with the exception of the little mass that protruded from my mid-section, but it had been enough to raise eyebrows in the last of my graduate courses at school. I quailed to think of myself in four months, ballooning from beneath a black graduation robe. We were wordlessly thrilled together, it seemed. "Girl," I whispered when his eyes asked the question.

"Girl," he repeated almost inaudibly, so full of wonder and what I could only understand as joy. I realized it had always been that way with us. He never withheld his joys from me, and I was only moderately careful with mine, hesitating only when I felt the fear creeping in. But Zach understood this about me and did not complain. Instead he quietly coaxed them from me with his love. If he felt fearful, he never showed it to me. Eclipsed by this shared happiness, the fact that I had sent him away five months earlier did not come up. It was understood, I felt, that I had never *not* wanted him. Never felt anything but gratitude for him in my life. That he was here now, his pure intent blazing in his green eyes, and that I had in my way asked him to be…it was enough.

Aware of my innate fears, Zach did everything to reassure me, to normalize what was to me the absolutely ab-normal business of having a human grow inside me, where I could not see to gauge whether what I was doing was well received or not. Did she like it when I ate Ignacio's "Supremely Spicy" salsa? Because it was all I wanted to eat. I think I would have eaten it with or without the tortilla chips. Did she feel soothed by the sensation of swimming in the pool at the "Y," or did she feel unmoored, frightened by the strangeness of being weightless within weightlessness? Did she like the sound of my singing, or was she sensitive to my vocal ineptitude and wishing I would be quiet?

And more importantly, did she already carry in her heart the seed of tragedy? The weakness that might leave her brittle and un-resilient in the face of loss? She came from a long line of fairly unstable women, it seemed to me. Was she to be, unwittingly, the extension of a hereditary cord of disillusionment and sadness passed on to her from her female predecessors, her own mother included? And that word! *Mother.* What weight. What gravity. How to be such a thing to a one so defenseless and without the capability to choose?

But Zach assured me that according to his belief, Azizah, for that is what we chose to name her, had *chosen* me. Before she ever took a body and began to grow inside me, she had made her choice, for both mother and father, based on all the ways she wanted to grow in this lifetime. This idea both calmed and alarmed me. It graciously removed some of the heaviness of my responsibility (if I turned out to be terrible at it, at least I could take comfort in thinking that perhaps in spirit Azizah had thought it would help her to have a terrible mother).

But it also raised questions about the heritage I must therefore have chosen for myself. Not only, said Zach, do we choose our parents, but we choose every struggle, every challenge we experience, which meant that rather than wondering *Why me?* in the face of adversity, one might ask, *What is it I intended to learn from this?* Approaching life and one's struggles from this perspective, rather than falling victim to self-pity and blaming, one might enter into the active endeavor of seeking some mystically intentioned growth. One might understand her suffering as self-selected, an act of courage, in the interest in grooming her spirit effectively. I loved this approach to understanding suffering; it resonated with some of the Buddhist teachings I had been exploring. The problem was that like those teachings, I found this perfect idea *imperfect* in its execution. Or, more specifically, I found *myself* imperfect in my efforts to execute it. When I thought of Adrian's mother, of the possibility of myself someday experiencing the grief that was hers, I did not feel enlightened or accepting of our *fates.* I just felt afraid.

With the imminent birth of a daughter in my very near future, these thoughts occupied my mind when it was not otherwise occupied with writing my creative thesis or analyzing French or Russian literature. Zach had let me choose the name Azizah, the origin of which was Hebrew meaning "powerful and strong." A lover of language, I suppose my hope was that her name might become a self-fulfilling prophecy and could somehow protect her from her dubious female lineage. We shortened it to "Zee" before she was ever born, but the intention was there, and it was never far from my mind.

Zach had begun taking photographs for *Extreme Sportsman Magazine* more regularly again, though still on a freelance basis. It was not the art that he had been on course to produce, but it felt like the right thing to do, and he seemed happy. All I could muster was the consciousness to eat healthily while I labored at the writing of my creative thesis. It would be the basis for my first book of poems, which Zach and I would later joke was my "firstborn child," Zee's fraternal twin, as it were. The last weeks of the pregnancy and of school were long and slow and filled with as much sleep as I could justify. I was so tired, and Zach would climb into the bed with me, cradle my body in his (with the new shape of my body, it was possible to *spoon* me from the front or back), and together we would dream of the moment our baby would enter the air and our lives in a more tangible way.

I could not really think beyond that, though my apprehension around giving birth was taking a pretty prevalent place in my mind. "Shhhh," Zach would say, and somewhere in my memory, though it soothed me, there was also the echo of my grandmother's "Shhh" and her unwillingness to acknowledge our shared history. There was the echo of her unwillingness to give me any inkling of whether the story I invented for her was anything like the reality that had engendered my father, me, and now my own daughter. There was the echo of Zee's heritage as only a fiction, something I could not in earnest hand down to her, having conceived its stories myself, fleshed them out with nuances and details that grew in my imagination from the skeletal truths I had been given.

August 1995, San Luis Obispo, California

On August 1st, 1995, six weeks after I completed my MFA and lumbered across the stage in the Cal Poly gymnasium, looking not unlike a black-gowned zephyr, I gave birth to Azizah Carroll Crane. I labored for twelve hours, most of which time I spent curled into a ball and clinging to the metal side rail of my hospital bed, moaning like a Wookie. I was "giving voice to my breath" as I had been advised to do by the various natural birthing books I had pondered in the weeks before the birth.

"Are you sure that's my sister in there?" I had heard my brother Robby ask from the doorway of my room, "and not Chewbacca?" It did not elicit laughter on my part at the time, but it became a favorite and enduring Zee birth quote in our family. In the moment he uttered it, I had wanted to punch him in the nose, but later, softened by memory and the gracious amnesia of post-birthing, I would remember it fondly. I would picture Robby there, leaning on the doorframe of my room, his floppy hair just brushing the eyelashes of his right eye. He would wink at the nurse who, though twice his age, could not help but blush at his Carroll charm and the attention he gave her.

The experience had been surreal and though I had been afraid, I was also aware of the miracle of what I was doing, of how it changed me, legitimized me as a woman somehow. Even in the months preceding the birth, I had noticed a change in the way women treated me, other women who were mothers; it was as if I had gained entrance into a secret society of women whose shared experience of motherhood dissolved the traditional boundaries of competitive female interaction. It was a bonus, so to speak, that I had not sought but which was conferred on me nonetheless.

Zee came out of me howling and pink, not like the babies I had seen born in the birth videos of our prenatal classes. I had prepared myself for a blue, still, strange looking entity. Instead, out came Azizah, bearing all the traits that her name connoted, ruddy and kicking and peeing, actually, as they laid her on my chest and allowed me to embrace her. The first "Apgar Ten" of my nurse's fifteen-year career, she would announce later. Little warrior, "powerful and strong."

"I love her!" was the thing that spilled from my lips, as if I had won a prize at the fair, and I began to cry as I held her. Not from sadness but from exhaustion, from gratitude, and from the awareness that I swear entered my consciousness with utter lucidity in the moment I first held her: that I would have to let her go someday.

Zach had held my hands, massaged my lower back, rubbed lavender into my temples and wrists, and done virtually everything that was requested of him for twelve hours straight. There was the strain, too, sometimes I think greater than the strain of the actual pain to bear, of watching the one he loved suffer for so long and feeling himself helpless against what seemed to turn my body inside out. He, too, was exhausted and wept as we made a nest around Zee with our bodies there on the hospital bed and she nursed for the first time. It was a kind of union I could not have understood apart from the experience of it. It was a yoking of two humans to the third human whom their love had yielded like a gift. I felt spent but also full of bliss.

It was a strange sensation perhaps beyond words, but in that moment, I could not imagine turning away from Azizah, could not imagine not putting my hands on her face when it was near, not wanting her again and again with this kind of fierceness, this kind of intensity. As I lay there contemplating these things into my sleep, I thought of my father as an infant. I saw him wriggling in Violet's arms, arms that would soon fail to catch him up in their embrace, and my first true milk came in. It was painful and deeply satisfying, my breasts swelling with its nourishment and with my intention not to repeat a history I was not sure I could escape but which I would resist with my entire body and for the remainder of my life.

Chapter Nine

July 1971, Turlock, California

When I was born, my mother and father had been married for a year and a half. My father was only twenty-one, my mother only nineteen when, their infant girl just three weeks old, they were called upon to 'deal with' Violet. In five years my father Matthew Carroll had not been back to the house he had left resolutely and with a plan. He was knee deep in his graduate studies, which occupied his nights. By day, he worked at the same cannery that had employed his mother during those first grim years in Turlock. Now, he and Lucinda Johnson, his high school sweetheart, were "playing house" in the country, raising two Irish Setters and a baby girl, biding their time until his dreams of becoming a college professor might come to fruition.

Lucinda, or Lucy as she was called, was seventeen years old ("lacked a month of being eighteen," as my grandmother put it) when she married my father and became a Carroll. She came from a long line of dairy farmers, displaced from Oklahoma by the Dust Bowl, and was the oldest bride in the Johnson family in four generations. For the first six months of their marriage, Matthew would set the alarm for himself at five, so that he could get in a few hours of studying before work at the cannery, and wake Lucy at seven for her last semester of high school. She graduated with honors from Turlock High School in June of 1970, and the very next year in July gave birth to me.

I think I must have been a surprise, though my powers of invention fail me here. Perhaps it is because I want so, even now, to believe that I was wanted from the beginning. Why is there always such a fine line in the mind between unplanned and unwanted? I did not fail to see the similarities between Zee's conception and my own, and yet the question remained. In any case, it would be six years before Lucy would conceive again and give birth to my brother Robby at the much more reasonable age of twenty-five.

Lucy was a petite girl with black hair like Violet's. Bizarrely, she too was of Cherokee and Irish descent. It was an unlikely combination unless you considered that these two groups represented two of the lower echelons of American society during the 19th century. They must naturally have gravitated toward one another, both of them trying to integrate with the society at large. Lucy's family tree is filled with "Cherokee women," none deemed important enough by the record keepers to name; thus it is only the Irish names of her family that have survived the strain of time's passage and the subjectivity of its historians.

Lucy's deep brown eyes and straight black hair had captivated Matthew the first time he saw her. That was when she was only fourteen and he seventeen. He had met her at a dance in town and liked her sassiness immediately. She had not betrayed her attraction for him right away, already versed as she was in the art of coquetry, thanks to her equally beautiful mother. In her Capri pants and Keds, she was a vision, her small breasts just budding beneath the pale fabric of her sweater set. He was entranced by her smooth, brown skin and the way she tilted her head to the side, as if to size him up, when he approached her. When they slow danced to "I Can't Stop Lovin' You" by Ray Charles, and Matthew smelled Lucy's strawberry scented hair, it pretty much sealed the deal.

They had spent the rest of the evening together, and then they had dated for a few months before Matthew had to leave for Conway and for the plans he had laid for himself the previous year when he was there for his brother's funeral. He was serious about the college thing and though he was already feeling the early pangs of love, Lucy was only fourteen and would be in high school for three years yet. They wrote a few letters after he left, but the distance had been great, and they had lost touch for a time, though Lucy had never been far from his mind.

It was not until he returned from school in Arkansas, transferring to Stanislaus State, that Matthew proposed to the fresh-faced girl. He indignantly demanded that she choose between a boy named Gill, whom she had been carelessly dating, and himself, returned to claim her. Lucy had giggled at his grandiosity, the boldness of his demand, knowing full well what a small thing he asked of her. She had pined for him for the last three years, only taking various beaus to distract her from her youthful longing. Poor Gill, the son of the local postman, never had a chance against the dangerous, handsome boy she had met at a dance so long ago and whose name had been on her tongue ever since.

Once, late at night with cotton balls between her pink-nailed toes, her hair rolled into fat blue curlers, Lucy had played at the Ouija board with her friends, and when asked who loved her, it had spelled out M-a-t-t-h-e-w. The girls had giggled madly and all sworn that they had not directed the game piece toward these letters. They had fallen into a heap of floral-print nightgowns on her bedroom floor, each of them sighing and dreaming of the boy who had her own heart at the time. Lucy had dreamed her wedding with Matthew a thousand times since then, and though she made him wait an excruciating minute and a half while she "considered," her heart's acceptance of his offer of love was immediate.

It was Hedda James who called Matthew and Lucy that late July morning. They had heard that Randall Pruitt had died in Violet's arms on a sunny spring day the year before. He had collapsed on the cracked cement walkway from driveway to front door, and Violet had caught him up awkwardly in her arms, his weight dragging them both onto the unkempt green lawn. Violet had not cried or uttered a sound, and it had been the neighbors who called for an ambulance, though Randall had died almost instantly from a massive heart attack. Years of abusing his body with food and too much drink had finally occluded the arteries around his heart, and he had left Violet with two words to carry into the eternity of her long life: *Help me.* The irony of his request was not lost on the woman who had been incapable even of helping herself for the last two decades.

Hedda James lived across the street from Violet and checked in on her from time to time. Violet was living on Randall's pension and had been taking care of their two little girls the best she could. Amelia was five now and Heather nearly four. Violet had not answered the phone and was not receiving visitors, but Mrs. James had looked in on her a few days ago, and again this morning. Both times Violet had been lying on the couch, listless, the girls moving around her and basically fending for themselves, and could Matthew please come and see what there was to be done.

Matthew knew there was no one else, Baby having moved back to Conway to work for Uncle Lawrence, and so he packed Lucy and the baby into their cream-colored Nova and drove out to the old farmhouse beneath gathering rain clouds. Lucy gently rocked the baby girl whom they had named Meghann Faye after Lucy's mother, and the young woman clucked and cooed softly to her, watching through the rainy windshield as Matthew made his way to the front door.

It was some time before he emerged again, and when he did it was to direct the ambulance drivers. Violet was not ill but unresponsive, lying still and silent beneath a sheath of newspapers on the couch, her salt-and-pepper hair rising like a wild halo around her head. About the same time that the ambulance arrived, so did Heather and Amelia's Aunt Elizabeth. Another benevolent sister. She wore a pillbox hat, somewhat out of fashion but matching with her purse and shoes and perfectly in keeping with her stern propriety. She quickly softened when she saw Matthew, forlorn and somewhat in shock where he stood on the porch, watching the emergency technicians assess his bewildered mother.

Aunt Elizabeth took the girls that day, pushed her husband's business card into Matthew's hand as she left with them. Inside the house, Matthew had found Heather in a sundress and no panties, Amelia standing on a chair with a hot iron at the ironing board, both of their faces dirty and gaunt. Matthew kissed the girls as they moved past him as if in slow motion or under water, while in his head he chastised himself for having been so remiss. But how could he have known that while in his own little home love was blooming into the careful nurturance of a daughter, these two daughters, his own half sisters, were raising themselves in his mother's virtual absence, the only thing she could ever really be counted on to produce?

It would be three months before Violet would be released from the Psych Ward at Middlefield General Hospital, but Matthew would never forget her face beneath the wild mass of her graying hair, her feral eyes, seemingly all pupil, as she was taken up into the ambulance that day. "I never knew you," she hissed at him through clenched teeth in the greatest display of emotion he could remember having witnessed from her in his life. It was not a revelation of any sort and yet it smarted, and he recoiled from the words as if they had form.

He stood there in the street as the ambulance pulled away, the neighbor's small white dog sniffing at his shoes as the rain continued to fall. Lucy watched him from the front seat of the car, as she nursed her baby girl and sang a Celtic lullaby, softly, softly. He stood there a long time, well after the ambulance had disappeared around a corner and the neighbors had lost interest, gone back inside their houses.

The rain came in giant drops, almost comical in their hugeness, soaking Matthew completely within moments. He sent a hand through his hair and then clasped both hands behind his head, shirttails coming out of his pants. He gazed for what felt like an infinite moment in the direction the ambulance had gone and then back at the house from which the morning's menagerie had issued. It was a life that had been his, for sure, but which he had managed to set apart from his young wife and even from himself. Undeniably, it still belonged to him, because while you can never go home again, you can never leave it entirely behind either.

It is a story I build from the little I know of how my grandmother came to be committed, the last two of her children removed from her custody. The poem, soon after Zee was born, wrote itself:

I never knew you, she said, and it was the truth. My dad was steady,
didn't cry. I imagine him quiet that day, sullen, as they closed
the door after her, trailing her pink terrycloth robe. You're never ready
to rethink the ridiculous. As they drove away, he stood in the road,

documents crumpled in his hand, white dog sniffing at his shoes. He
had not been back to the old house, and he looked to it now, thrown
against sky and still leaning uncomfortably, sighing his scattered family.
His daughter had her eyes, and a tuft of her black hair, a crown

of memory. He had always known that the past was inescapable,
and yet he ran, pausing only to breathe an ellipsis into recollection. They
would have no words for that moment. She would return, too, unable
to remember or speak what had been. She would place a glass ashtray

on the arm of the sofa, a sweating glass of iced tea on a metal coaster,
and fade into the yellowed walls of that house as it gently forgave
her.

Chapter Ten

August 1995, San Luis Obispo, California

Everyone in my family welcomed Zee into the clan, and Zach's family, though scattered from Figi to San Diego, did too. She was the bright and beautiful product of a union that had grown organically of its own accord, fate pushing us around a bit, it seemed, for our own good. I occupied myself very much with Zee's care in those early days of living with Zach. It had just happened naturally that we would live as a family, and while Zach had known that I was not ready to talk about marriage, the rest of the family was clamoring with the question. Even my brother had razzed me, his conventional sister, for having such an "unconventional" arrangement, but I did not allow these things to penetrate the hard shell of my immediate concern:

caring for a newborn on limited sleep and with limited resources.

I was trying, too, to get a job teaching at Cuesta College, but I knew that the publication of my first book of poems would open that door much more than would my fresh graduate degree. In the hours that Zee slept, I wrote, as long as I could stay awake; I generated, tweaked and revised, and I swam around in the liquid matter of my language. Zee and my poetry kept me enough removed from the mundanity of every day life, that I could essentially mute the question of how to proceed with Zach. While he did not pressure me, I felt a tension rising in our conversation, sparse as it was, and in the space that grew between us in our bed.

It happened that a huge chunk of the book I was working on had been derived during the years following Adrian's death. It was in many ways because of the distance, both in terms of time and emotion, that I was able to craft poems on the subject. My early writings about Adrian had amounted to a whole lot of emotionally charged drivel. When I had found, during my last year of graduate school, that I could contain the wildness of the dominant emotion surrounding that topic through the use of formal verse, I had returned to the subject of Adrian and his family with renewed intensity. Of course it appeared from the outside that I was fixating on him and on the loss. Though I felt I knew otherwise, I was irritated by the suggestion and obstinately refused to explain myself and what I was up to in crafting new poems on a subject I had at one time abandoned.

It was about creating something beautiful from the destruction of an unwelcome 'change' in my life. It was about manifesting the creator in me, building art from ruins, writing something, finally, that had literary merit where once there had been only wildness and undisciplined verbiage. And the parallel task: growing a child with my love. I did not believe it was possible to spoil a baby, and so I doted on Zee, gave her everything I could understand that she wanted and more. Zach, on the other hand, I kept outside of the circle of my affection. With my refusal to explain the *why* of my newly rekindled interest in the subject of Adrian, he felt wounded, and rather than spark my compassion, it hardened me against him. It was a kind of defensiveness I have a hard time understanding, even now, but it was real, and it separated us.

I let Zee sleep with me, barely waking for night feedings, when she would root her way to my body and take my breast in her greedy little blossom of a mouth, drink until she slept again, surfeited with my love. She lived her first months in a wrap I had devised with long swathes of fabric from South America. She moved as I did, accompanying me at every task. When she tired of my body's warmth and preferred instead to observe the world around her, I strapped her to my back in the same textiles, her little fists hanging over one of my shoulders while her eyes, glossy in their blackness, swept the space, taking in everything they could.

There was little room or time for Zach in my days, and though he would occasionally invite me to take Zee for a walk with him, bundle her from head to toe in organic cottons and Merino wool to explore the environs of San Luis Obispo or Morro Bay, mostly he was at a loss. I suppose I felt consumed with nurturing my two 'babies' and was somewhat annoyed by needs less demanding but present nonetheless and voiced by a full-grown man. I needed his help with the laundry, endless mounds of baby garments and diapers and blankets, and with the dishes, spilling from our sink endlessly. I had no interest in considering my body as sensual, as my own; it had become the source of Zee's sustenance and nothing more. Though Zach might touch my face or push a stray lock of my hair behind my ear, I would not respond, would shrug off his attentions as superfluous. Self-indulgent. It was a kind of Spartan self-discipline that hurt us both.

I needed Zach to support me in the work of raising our baby, and I was only willing to acknowledge his equivalent needs. Nothing beyond that could be acknowledged, and this was a function of my limited scope of awareness. Perhaps I was sabotaging our relationship; perhaps I was choosing one kind of vulnerability over another, feeling inadequate for giving myself to more than one person at a time. Perhaps there still lurked the fact that what had brought Zach back to California, had inspired my invitation, was my pregnancy with Zee. Whatever it was, it served to create a large crevasse between us, one that finally became impassable, it seemed. The more I resisted Zach's entrance into the circle I had drawn around Zee and myself, the less he seemed to desire it, and he began to spend many hours 'on assignment' and in his makeshift darkroom in the basement.

One evening over dinner, there was almost a conversation, at last. Dinner was a vegetarian pizza we had made from scratch, together in a window of closeness inspired perhaps by a rainy day and nursing Zee, who had caught a cold. "How are the photos coming?" I asked tentatively. Zach was working on an assignment that involved a group of back-country skiers.

"They're good. Caught the light just right," he said between bites. There was a dampness to his expression and his tone that I could only interpret as disappointment. It was so subtle, so fine and, looking back, likely enhanced by my own feelings of guilt.

"It's a good project, Zach." My voice was flat.

"I know. And it's good money."

"That we need."

"Mmmm," he intoned around a bite of bell pepper, carmelized onion and mozzarella cheese. I sat quietly for a bit, my appetite having left the way of my sensitivity toward Zach's need to create. How could I not acknowledge the same impulse in him to be involved, deeply, in a creative project, in his art? But it was so: I could not. I could only feel the rising bitterness of exhaustion and feeling pulled in more directions than I could accommodate.

"Look, if it's too much—"

"Too much?" he said, incredulous. "What are you talking about, Meg? Sometimes I think you want me to give up."

"Whoah, geez. Touchy much?"

"Oh, come on. It's always right there. You suggesting that we throw in the towel. I know you, Meg. I know this is an effort for you. I don't know why, but I know that it is."

"*This*?"

"Yeah, this. Being together. Being a couple. With Zee."

"I'm perfect with Zee," I said.

"Yes, I know. I love that you're *perfect* with Zee," he said, almost pleading.

"But what?"

"But nothing," he said. Like that, we skirted the subject. Again and again, we would start to talk about something real, my defenses would rise, and Zach would back down. Why he did not call me on my selfishness I do not know. Perhaps it would have only blown sky high, and he somehow knew that. Perhaps it was an expression of his patience. His willingness to wait out my self-indulgence. I seemed to be still nursing old wounds, still precariously balanced on a fence that separated my real life from the life of my dreams, the life of my Violet-self, where I slid through the ether in search of one who was long gone from me and would not return.

That was an incredibly prolific period of Zach's career, and the photos that issued from that space and time were amazing, though they were bound by assignments and stories that were far from what stirred in his artist heart.

Sometimes he would have to go on trips to photograph athletes or events, and Zee and I would be left to our quiet reveries. One less person to pick up after, I remember having thought, for so a man's presence is often reduced by the consciousness of a young mother. Less laundry, fewer dishes, less food to cook. In the absence of emotional support, which I had been quick to resist, these were what remained of our partnership. At twenty-four, I could not see beyond these limitations, and I was certainly incapable of recalling what had bound us to one another beyond the brilliant little life we had together created.

When my book was published at the time of Zee's first birthday, I was feeling pretty invincible. *Stellar Decline* was picked up by Darjeeling Press, edited by a friend of a friend from my MFA program, and though its initial press run of two thousand was modest, I felt I had arrived on some level and that I could keep going at this rate. Zee and I spent our days ambling to the park or walking on the beach at Morro Bay, for there she had taken her first steps at only eleven months, while Zach shot multiple photographs and we both laughed deliciously. They were moments that had given me reason to think about the man who, I knew, was patiently waiting for something to shift in me, but I had been careless, and I let the moments go.

I took a job at Cuesta College teaching composition courses to a mixed bag of students; I had everything from over-privileged but underachieving coeds to middle-aged women returning to school after the detritus of raising a family had cleared from their lives. They had been left with empty nests and the impulse to resist Voltaire's third great evil: boredom. Not exactly what I had envisioned for myself and a far cry from the distinguished career of my father, but it was a start, and I was young. My father had recently received the award for Distinguished Faculty of the Year at the University of California at Santa Cruz, where he had taught for nearly thirty years and regularly published his scholarly work on the writings of the early Americans. He was my inspiration, though I was inclined toward the creative, while his arena was that of literary criticism. MFA versus PhD, the perennial divide among the faculty of the institutions of higher learning. I had nowhere to go but up, I thought then, and I threw myself into my teaching the way I did my poetry and the "loving up" of my daughter.

One afternoon after my Freshman Composition class, an intrepid boy approached me. I had given him a fairly harsh grade on a paper that was exquisite for the first page and mediocre at best for the next three. He sauntered over to where I sat working and dropped the paper, pushed it toward me on my desk. The pages were folded over their staple and open to the comment in my unmistakable teacher's scrawl: "You blew your wad on the first page. If you could sustain the energy and intellect you expended to develop that, then we'd be in business." I was a little embarrassed. It was, in fact, a pretty inappropriate thing to write on a student's paper. And it was followed by a large, circled C-minus. A sheepish kind of response came to my lips, something about how it had been late when I had graded it and how I had been frustrated by the drivel I had been reading all evening, but when I met his eyes with mine, I did not speak. His grey eyes were soft and had a smile in them. He obviously thought it was funny, but he was not backing down.

"Chase--"

"Meghann." It was the first time he had spoken my name, and it arrested me. I *had* chosen to go by my first name with my students. I was not a "doctor" after all, but a writer and an instructor. Ms. Carroll had sounded like a grade school teacher and was frumpy in my ear. So Meghann it had been, but they rarely called me by name. And this boy. My name was lovely coming from his mouth, I remember thinking.

"I rewrote it," he said, his face now breaking into a wide grin as he handed me another draft.

"Oh, okay-- good," I said. "I'm glad you did, Chase." He was a kid I had seen in the water on a few of the rare occasions I had gotten myself out to surf since Zee had been born. Always alone, of course, because me surfing meant Zach on baby detail. Zach and I had fallen into a pattern of mutual parenting, the shared free time that had given rise to our love having dissolved into the new schedule of trading off caring for Zee. It was a common trap of young parents, and I see now that had I been aware of it, I might have countered it, but the problem between us ran deeper than that. It was the gulf of my own emotional distance. I had receded into that stellar space just out of reach. At home, I was Zee's mother, and at work, I was some detached version of myself, someone beloved of a young group of students, someone young and free and beautiful in a way I did not feel at home, wearing spit-up on my shoulder and nursing pads in my bra.

I became aware for a moment that this boy saw me the way I saw myself when I was there at school, or better, when I was in the water doing what I had done as a girl. Riding waves and communing with the sea. Though I did not admit it to myself at the time, at least in this moment, this boy must also have seen me as Adrian had. "You'll read it?" he asked, eyebrows raised slightly.

"Of course I'll read it. I always want to reward the work that you do. You took the time to write it, I'll read it." When he stood still, seeming to wait for me to finish, I added, "And I'll grade it."

"Sweet."

"Yeah, sweet," I said, adding the paper to the enormous stack of essays I had yet to grade that day. "Only the new grade won't replace the old; they'll be averaged. Fair?"

"Fair," he said, winking at me in a highly disconcerting way. One more winning smile and he was out the door. I sat with my hands limp in my lap, considering the exchange.

It was one that gave me pause. Not because I had been attracted, even mildly, to a boy eight years my junior and enrolled in my Freshman Composition course. Not because I thought I would ever let that feeling toward Chase Everett stir in me again. But because it signified something that was latent in me, some desire to feel like I had when I was eighteen, before Adrian had died.

I was hardly old. And I could easily have dismissed it as the common mania of young mothers, who find themselves suddenly desirous to be sexy, wild, even dangerous, but separate from the nest of house and home that they have built, because the feeling is so contrary to that enterprise. It passes, almost invariably, but it gives young fathers a pretty good scare if they perceive it. That was not it, though. Somewhere in me, I knew what it was. It had to do with a deep hole I was still trying to fill, only my selectiveness, my resistance to Zach in particular, was making it hard and skewing the effort.

Later that night, when an argument between me and Zach had reached its fever pitch, Zach had exclaimed out of the blue, "Meg, I can't compete with a dead guy!" I had slammed the door against his ridiculous non sequitur, but I had listened with my body pressed against it as he went on.

"In death he becomes perfect. Don't you think I know that? How can I compete with a guy who can never make another mistake again?" It seemed ludicrous to me, for Adrian was far from my conscious thoughts. If Zach had any real idea of what had gone through my head that afternoon, he would have been furious. Pining after a lost lover was one thing. It was weak and pathetic maybe. But it was not salacious. Something in me crumbled when I heard Zach say the words. Not because I had briefly lusted after an eighteen-year-old boy who was my educational charge, but because in my heart I knew Zach was right. I was still looking for Adrian. Moments like those in my office with Chase Everett felt like I had found him, if only for a moment, and being with some version of Adrian meant being who I was when I was with him. Someone beautiful and untamed. Someone lovely and bound by nothing. Someone whole.

I was broken, it seemed, haunted by a shadow past. I had not held Zach up to the image of Adrian, but I had kept him far from me, preferring fantasy over reality. It was not a conscious choice but one that had grown out of habit and was complicated by our long absences from one another and the necessity of living our lives out separately, even while we slept under the same roof, shared the same bed. Sitting there, huddled at the base of the door, I had a strange experience. I felt a little dizzy, and I was having trouble breathing.

"Are you okay?" Zach said from the other side of the door.

"No."

"Open the door, Meg," he said, his voice becoming tense. "Do you have Zee?" I nodded, as if he could see me, and Zee toddled over and climbed into my lap. She tucked my braid behind her ear as she always did, began to suck her thumb and pressed her head against my chest. She was listening to my heartbeat, which seemed to me to be sputtering and unreliable. I was so tired all of a sudden, and I could not "see to see." I closed my eyes against the feeling of disorientation, of weightlessness, as if I had suddenly become insubstantial.

Behind my eyelids appeared a waking dream. Behind my body and the door, I could hear Zach fiddling with the lock, but that sound grew distant as the image in my mind's eye came into focus. It was a parade of women, no-- a finite but repeating procession, all of them with black braided hair like mine. All of them moving as if underwater. All of them wearing the strain of disappointment and grief on their taut faces: Grandma Virgilia, Dolores, Violet, myself in effigy.

I struggled against the image, but it continued relentlessly until Grandma Virgilia in her lavender dress, sleeves fluttering on an imaginary wind, turned to face me. I could see that her dress was open to the waist and she had a small child at her breast. When the child lifted her face from Virgilia's body, I saw that it was Zee. The older woman's breast fell from her mouth in a torrent of toxic green liquid, and Zee wiped its excess from her chin with the back of her plump little hand.

I shrieked aloud, startling Zee in my lap and impelling Zach, who had managed the lock with a bobby pin, to begin pushing the door open against my frozen body. I moved away to allow his entrance, only barely aware of where I was or what I did, and the first thing he did was scoop Zee from my arms. I was pale and trembling, and I had no words to give him. Zee was wailing uncontrollably, and Zach held her head to his chest, the way she had laid it on mine, his hand over her ear as if to shield her from her own cries. He looked at me like I had hurt her. There was fear in his expression. And a fine layer of disdain.

Chapter Eleven

September 1998, San Luis Obispo

In the fall of 1998, shortly after Zee turned three, I received a letter in the mail. It had been forwarded from my father, who had chosen not to open it. It was from the Joint POW/MIA Accounting Command (JPAC) at Hickam Air Force Base in Honolulu, Hawaii. It said that the dog tag finding back in 1990 had precipitated a more aggressive investigation of my grandfather's case. As cooperation had grown between the U.S. and Russian governments, a Korean War Working Group of the Joint Commission Support Directorate between the two countries had worked to gain access to the Ministry of Defense archives at Podolsk. One of their finds had been a report filed by a Russian aviator that referenced the shoot down of an

American F-86 near Antung (Dandong) on September 12th, 1952.

My father, knowing the content of the letter, had sent it along to me, the family member most likely to have interest in this sort of thing. Matthew Carroll had grown up without a father. For him, the story ended there. He did not want to know why his mother had emotionally vacated her body at intervals, so that he and his two brothers, and subsequently four half siblings, would be left to fend for themselves or be rescued ignominiously by various outside relatives. He paid his obligatory visits to her in her dark farmhouse in Turlock, California twice a year. A good son, he spent thirty-five minutes in her presence, every July and December. He would semi-annually ignore the dearth of human sensation between himself and his mother, the vacant expression in her eyes, her jaw set against acknowledgment of what was shared in their history.

This, a letter suggesting new intelligence regarding his father's disappearance back in 1952, was an interruption to the resignation he had cultivated during his entire adult life. When his daughter was born in 1971, he had shifted his focus toward the family he would build with his young wife. Together they would supplant the void of familial experience that had been his for as long as he could remember. Together they would become the Carroll family.

During the quarter century since he had committed his mother to an asylum, a profound admission of his helplessness where her mental instability was concerned, Matthew Carroll had nurtured a beautiful family. He had become a distinguished professor at a university in the Bay Area of northern California, had published multiple papers on various literary topics, and had loved his wife through two bouts of breast cancer. His daughter, though sometimes her eyes flickered with the same doubt he saw in his mother's eyes, was also accomplished, a published poet at twenty-seven and a budding educator.

His son Robby was accomplished, as well. He had graduated valedictorian of his high school and now studied pre-med at the University of California at Davis. This was what the Carrolls had become. Matthew's brothers had gone their ways. Ricky into the sky after their pilot father, Sebastian to Arkansas to live alongside the only father figure he had ever known, coaxing crops from the earth and marrying a girl from Conway. He too was extending a new strand of Carrolls into the world, connecting them with those extending from Uncle Lawrence and Uncle Eddie. Cousins who were also part of the shadow past Sebastian carried in his heart as the blueprint for the way he would grow his own family.

My father had grown up without a father, and the story for him ended there. My Uncle Seb had followed up to a certain extent with the JPAC team and their communications, but when the letter came inviting the Carroll boys to the Central Identification Laboratory in Honolulu to claim the remains of their father and escort them to the cemetery of their choice, the brothers were at a loss.

There had been an archeological expedition to China and the exchange of intelligence among three countries who until then had guarded a keen silence. There had passed into American hands the actual dog tags of Charlie Carroll, and now after nearly a year of requisite testing, including a DNA sample provided by Uncle Eddie, this: the positive identification of two Ziploc bags worth of human remains, fished from beneath a Chinese man's penjing studio, as Captain Robert Charles Carroll of the U.S. Air Force Reserve.

The military would pay for two family members to fly to Honolulu to perform the customary rites and escort his remains finally to his resting place on American soil, which would inevitably be at the Oak Grove Cemetery in Conway, Arkansas. He would be laid next to his son and next to his oldest brother Russell, who had also served in the war as a pilot and then lived twenty more years before dying in a car crash. Zach had raised his eyebrows at my insistence on being one of the two family members to go, but he knew that it was something I needed to do, and I wanted to do it *with* my father.

"I don't know, Meggie," my dad had said on the phone that night, but we both knew he would go. That here was closure not hoped for. Truth relinquished long ago but offering itself now unflinchingly. Uncle Seb was happy to greet us at the airport in Little Rock if the two of us wanted to fly to Honolulu and take care of matters on that end. As I stood and discussed these things quietly with my father, Zee laughed, tangled in the spiral cord of my old fashioned telephone. I pushed black strands of hair from her face, knowing that this trip would come at a critical time for me and Zach. I wondered how the thing would unravel, for surely it would under the relentless influence of passing time.

The last two years had been strained, and it turned out that it did matter that I had sent Zach away originally, had refused his offer to stay when the only reason to stay was our desire to be together. Our love, unnamed as it was. It came up in argument after argument, and always in the form of a question: "Did you even want me to come back?" It was a fair question, though I thought I had made it clear at the time. I had to admit now that the Rilke poem was less than definitive, but then again, hadn't Zach known me well enough, even then, to hear the invitation in the poem? "You certainly didn't want me when I was leaving," he would sometimes add or, "You've always known exactly what you wanted; I don't know what makes me think that I will suddenly become a part of that equation." These kinds of comments only weakened Zach in my mind. I think I wanted him to call me on being insensitive. On being a jerk, really. But he did not. Not once.

At the Santa Barbara airport that December, I wept as I put Zee on a plane with Zach, though I knew it was only for six days. They would fly to San Diego to spend the week with Zach's mother, who lived there alone and had been pining to see her granddaughter since her second birthday party in August. At the gate, Zach put Zee down and took up my hands in his. I felt a little awkward, because we had grown unaccustomed to such tenderness between us, but I allowed it. He looked at me searchingly, and I knew that there was something he had decided. Something he meant to ask of me for a change. He surprised me by speaking it now.

"Meg, you need to decide. I want you. That is sure. But you need to decide if you want me."

"I want Zee," I blurted.

"I know," he said. "And she wants you. We have clarity there." I breathed a little easier then, but waited for Zach to close in on what I knew now that he meant to say.

"If you love me, then let's try." It was simple. It was compassionate. "But if you don't, I think it's not fair to anyone for us to continue like this." I looked at him then. Observed his fine features. His green eyes and his bleached out fall of brown hair. I looked at his expression, the deep longing there. He loved me. I could see that. I had hurt him. This I could also see. His voice moved around me like ocean waves. It was that sibilance of water over sand, the sound I loved.

"I don't know, Zach. I can't--" but he stopped me with a weak wave of his hand.

"Not right now, for God's sake," he said sadly. "When you get back. Take this time to think. Be with your family. Be with your dad. I'll be here with Zee when you return." I turned my head instinctively when he leaned to kiss me, so that his lips brushed only the corner of my mouth. Zee, who had been playing in the folds of my long, bohemian skirt, looked up at us now, a huge grin spread across her face. I lifted her to my hip and touched her neck with my forefinger, knowing her "ticklish spot." She ducked her chin and giggled, coming back up with her black eyes soft and open, her smile inherent inside them.

"I love you, baby girl," I whispered in her ear and kissed her cheek before handing her to Zach.

"I love you," he said to me, and though I did not look away, I could not return the words. I did not know how I felt, it had been so long since I had considered it. I had blocked the question from my mind for months, years it seemed. Did I love him? Was there love left over when I pulled back my myopic focus on my daughter? I had intentionally focused on her this way, I knew. I had closed in on her so as not to admit anything else. It was my way, I thought then. It was my limitation. Perhaps it was the pattern of my kind. Violet had focused so tightly on Charlie, or so I had dreamed it, that when he left her, bent the blue sky in his exit from our atmosphere, her capability to love collapsed, as if under some gravitational pressure, left her in the vacuum of her own want.

I would not lose Zee. It was inadmissible. It was unthinkable. Zach was now pressing in on me to decide something I had decided long ago but which had been thrown into confusion by his entrance into my world. I had decided, before I ever met him, not to give myself to anyone. And yet I had conceived Zee and loved her helplessly without my consent, as it were. With her, what was done was done, and I was inextricably bound by that love, by its accompanying fear. But I did not have to choose such a bond, such bondage, with anyone else if I did not want to.

Think. Yes, I would do that. I had a five-hour flight to Honolulu and an eight-hour one to Little Rock. These would be good thinking hours. And in between them I would tend to my own father, who would doubtless need my love in his own way.

December 1998, Honolulu, Hawaii

I met my dad in San Jose, and we flew together to Honolulu. Arrangements had been made for an Army escort out to Pearl Harbor. In the Oahu International Airport, a wiry young man with a neat blond flat-top held a small sign with our names and beckoned to us as we came off the plane there. It was strange to be treated with such decorum, as if the remains we were claiming were those of a brother or a son killed in Bosnia only last week. I felt a wave of gratitude that this was not the task before us, and yet it was with gravity still that we drove to the base with Officer Jay Houseman. He was in his blue service uniform and did not miss a single door as he ushered us on our way.

My dad was quiet, as usual, and he let me follow Officer Houseman into the Central Identification Laboratory on the Hickam Air Force Base (CILHI). We were greeted by a number of officers and Air Force higher ups and by

Sergeant Shanna O'Keefe who had taken lead on my grandfather's case. Shanna was young, maybe my own age, and she insisted that we call her by her first name. Her handshake was firm but gentle, her smile full of warmth and compassion. Regardless of how long this body had lain in the ground (nearly a half century at this point), it was the body of my father's father. What she held out to us was an ending to a story that had been abandoned, left unpunctuated by a conclusion or any kind of answer to a million questions that Matthew Carroll and his family had carried in their hearts for so many years. This is what she honored with her reverence.

Shanna, with her long red hair pulled back into a voluminous ponytail of curls that fell down the middle of her back, seemed the antithesis of the Air Force sergeant whose job it would be to guide us through the sterile laboratory and present us with the remains of "the deceased." The fine spray of freckles on her Irish face, her glimmering blue eyes and the dimple in the center of her chin gave her more the appearance of a pixie than a military official and immediately endeared her to my father, I could see.

He seemed more at ease in her presence, and his tension melted a little more with each smile she granted us, those effusive smiles balanced precisely with her professionalism and the gravity with which she approached the entire process. We followed "Sergeant Shanna" through a tour of the facility and finally into a large laboratory with steel gurneys laid out in neat rows. Each gurney bore a card with the identifying codes of the remains that were spread out on its expanse. On one gurney: a fragment of skull at the head of the gurney, a boot heel near the foot, several shattered ribs where one might presume the chest would fall, if a soldier's body were to be laid out on the steel bed.

These were the remains of soldiers who had yet to be identified, whose families still lived in the limbo of *not-knowing*. Had the mothers of those families lost their way, too? Had their lives splintered the way Virgilia and Violet's had when they got the un-news of their boys' absence? Not dead but "missing," not deceased but invisible. Floating in the space of their *not-knowing*, but completely unreachable as befits a true mystery. These soldiers were missing from as far back as World War I. The bowed head of the MIA/POW insignia, the silhouette of a man with a watchtower beyond him, took on new meaning. "You are not forgotten," whispers the banner. I had seen it on ball caps, on flags, even T-shirts. Not forgotten indeed.

The effort to identify these soldiers was vast and cost a fair amount of the Air Force's money, but it was a critical work in service to the families of the fallen. Many of them had been waiting as long as, or even longer, than we. When Sergeant Shanna led us to the gurney on which Charlie Carroll would be laid and wrapped in a wool blanket, a door at the back of the laboratory opened and through it we could see an ambulance. The remains were brought to us on a stretcher, though they fit inside of two large Ziploc storage bags, as delicately as if they comprised the intact body of a soldier who had died yesterday. I was struck by the decorum and the formality of the scene and by the way Sergeant Shanna removed one bit of bone at a time from its receptacle, gently, gently, laying the pieces out on the army green blanket, until both bags were empty.

When asked if we wanted to be left alone with the remains, I spoke up for my father who had been moved to speechlessness by the kindness of Shanna's act, by the import of what we did there, by the truth contained in these fragments, now dry and brittle, of what had once been a vibrant, breathing human body. "Yes," I said, and "please."

It felt strange to stand there with my father in our feigned privacy, for the entire south wall of the lab, behind which stood Sergeant Shanna O'Keefe and several others in white lab coats, was made of glass. Still, our backs were to them, and we were silent. What welled in me was myriad. It was the sorrow of four, even five generations over what I already knew to be the keenest kind of grief: the bewildering fact of a child dying before his mother. It was the torrential relief, also tearful, of *knowing*. Finally *knowing* the truth. Knowing that yes, my father's father had died there in that jet, the day he disappeared. That he was not floating somewhere in orbit around the planet of our denial, the denial of his people: father, mother, wife, brothers, children. Even grandchildren. It was the overwhelming sadness of knowing how we all die and worse: the people we love die, too. It was also the recurrent epiphany that my father grew up alone. Without a father and consequently, with a ghost of a mother.

We stood there weeping for a long time, and finally I noticed that my dad's hands were poised at his sides, fingers outstretched and trembling. "Do you want to touch him?" I asked, but I knew the answer to the question. Even I felt moved to touch this little that remained of my grandfather, but I did not dare. Apologetically, my dad looked at me, eyes red and glossy.

"If you never touched your dad, you know?" he said, as if to explain.

"Go ahead, Dad. It's okay." I spoke softly, urgently, and put my hand on his shoulder. As I did, he extended a hand to touch all that remained of his father, of the body that had engendered him, and through himself his own two children. That touch had to do with the million times he had wished as a child that his father was there to rumple his hair or pinch his cheek. The million ways he wished he could have touched his father in the years his mother fell to pieces in his absence. A handshake, a pat on the back, an encircling hug. His own hand on his father's aged one, as he lay dying…in the right order of things. In the right way of life moving as we live it, elders passing into the ether while their children usher them across the invisible threshold.

There were moments in the funeral home, too, where my grandfather's remains were taken in the ambulance from the base. In the laboratory, Sergeant Shanna and Officer Houseman had folded the blanket carefully over him, taken gold, oversized safety pins and moved spectrally around the gurney, inserting each pin with formality. Once, the sergeant had stopped, opened her hand over the young officer's work. He had halted and blushed deeply, for he understood his mistake immediately. He had inserted the pin in the wrong direction; sheepishly he corrected his work, and they had both continued in silence.

My grandfather's uniform was laid out inside an ornate rosewood coffin, lined with white satin. Beneath its hollow shell, we knew: those bits of the man who had spent the last forty-four years inside a wrecked cockpit. The patriarch of our family. My father's father. I laid violets across the torso of the uniform, quietly honoring my grandmother whom even my father could not bear to acknowledge now. She had defiled his memory, hadn't she? With her frailty and her searching. With the way she had squandered the life that was left to her after he died. With her failure to mother the children he had conceived with her. As far as my great uncles were concerned, she was no one. And now, with the truth of their brother's death so clear, so neatly explained, Violet, his wayward bride, would not be granted admittance into this anachronistic ceremony. They felt, understandably, that this forty-four-years-late closure was not hers to have. Not hers to know.

Of course I had gone to her. In the month before I went to San Jose to meet my father, I had loaded Zee into her great car seat and gone to Turlock to tell Grandma Esther everything. Even then I remember having anticipated the moment of my revelation. The clatter of my grandmother's silent resolve falling, as she opened herself to me, crying out, "I always knew, Meggie! I always knew." I anticipated the way I would collect her in my arms and absorb her grief, for once released and allowed to flow away from her aging body. Finally, we would touch, grandmother and granddaughter, united at last. Instead she had looked at me strangely, cocked her head to one side, and then gone back to watching a rerun of "Three's Company" on the television.

I had repeated myself, even planted myself between her and the TV, but she had looked through me, offered me an iced tea, rubbed one arthritic hand with the other. "Meggie," she had said to me, "do you think you can reach that box that's on top of the fridge? It's something Hedda brought by. I asked her to put it there, and I haven't been able to reach it since!" And she laughed heartily at this, sniffed, shifted her weight in her seat, before resuming her gaze at the TV screen. I paused, wordless and shrunken, my theories of her absolute love for Charlie Carroll dissipating into the theme song spilling into the room: *You can knock on my door. Come and ring on my bell.* I lifted the box from the top of the refrigerator and set it on the table: an assortment of party crackers. I opened them and gave one to Zee without asking.

When I left, Zee on my hip and carrying a deck of cards she had found on a side table, I suggested that we might write to one another, clinging still to the idea that Grandma Esther had something to impart to me and, unfathomably, a latent desire to do so. Perhaps in writing she would feel less inhibited. I had seen a letter she had written to my grandfather once. It was the only sample I had of her handwriting, but I knew that she had perfect penmanship and a deft mastery of the English language. Her sentences in that letter had been lilting, full of her sensuous voice, her keen intellect. Yes, perhaps we could write.

On the day that I left for San Jose, I had received a card in the mail. I recognized Violet's neat hand in an instant and tore open the envelope excitedly. Inside the envelope was a holiday greeting card, to my knowledge the first she had ever sent. There was a picture of the baby Jesus on the front, yellow light tinged with gold glitter pouring from his infant body in all directions. Inside, a scripted greeting about the season and adjacent, in Violet's penmanship, these words: *Sorry Meghann. I'm not one for writing. Love, Grandma Esther.*

Heritage

Some notion of our story is sung in the nod of her head,
soft pillow of opened palm, slow gesture of hand through
still air. I offer my daughter as proof of self, proof of said
connection and memory, though she is fair and soft, eyes too

blue green, their ocean not yet swallowed by doubt—whatever
it is that changes us. She's wearing an orange clip of yarn around
her thin, gray ponytail. It's almost as if with it I could tie up her
loveless drawl, the gentle distance between lips and the sound

uttered in the moments before death, soft exhalation of yes
and please. Almost worth looking for the skein. A tiny windmill
sits motionless on the porch. Made of waxed milk cartons, this
artifact is evidence of some creative streak. Or of the malignant

desire to flaunt the kind of boredom that chews at the heart, strange common trait, the way I have taken up crocheting, though it stultifies.

We had several hours to kill in Honolulu, and so my father and I enjoyed a meal together at the Hula Grill in Waikiki. The Air Force had put us up at the Outrigger, so it was an easy elevator ride to the restaurant. There we could sit and face the sea, be touched by ocean air and the sound of insistent little waves as we dined and spoke intermittently about inconsequential things. The weather in Santa Cruz, the difficulty of potty training a two-year-old, my dad's new Blue Heeler. The heaviness of our task hung in the air about our ears. It occasionally lighted on my dad's shoulders, at which time he seemed to shrug and send it away. We had always found it hard to talk about real things, though the connection between us was profound. Silence was our best mode together and finally, around the second course, we embraced it.

Beyond the long swathe of golden sand, waves broke in rapid succession, the long, shallow expanse of the Waikiki shoreline generating its famously gentle and consistent parade of waves. There were still people in the water, as darkness would not fall for another half hour yet, and "evening glass-off" was in full effect. The setting sun sent an orange cast over the bodies of the many surfers, most of them beginners, but some locals who knew where to sit to catch a wave that was a little steeper, a little faster, and which rose out of seeming nothingness. It was about knowing the ocean floor, the strategic positioning of one's board over a lone reef. Occasionally a delighted squeal or a hoot would punctuate the quiet air, and I felt a pang of jealousy, but this was not a surf trip. In fact, my dad was looking levelly at me now, poised to speak. Finally he broke the silence we had kept for most of the meal.

"Meg, how are things? With you and Zach." He asked the question rather sheepishly but did not back down, probably out of some paternal obligation he was feeling.

"We're fine, Dad. Why?" I did my best to look casual. This trip was about him, not me.

"No reason," he said quickly, "I just..." And his eyes shifted from my face to the candle on the table where the waiter was struggling with a lighter, and back to my face again.

"Really, Dad. I mean, it's hard, you know? With Zee. My job. I don't know."

"It's work, Meg. A marriage."

"Dad, you know we're not married."

"Aren't you?" he said. It was symbols that had meaning for my dad. It was something we had in common.

"I suppose that's what I'm meant to decide. This week. Ha ha," I said weakly, my eyebrows inching toward one another in a small frown as I sent my gaze out across the water.

"Try to remember," is all he said, but I knew what he meant. It was true that I had forgotten what had made me fall into Zach, trust him with my life, agree to raise a baby with him. At some point I had wanted to be his. Had as much as given myself to him. But I could not recall the accompanying feeling. Could not remember loving him like that. My thoughts toward him had been dominated for so long by the suspicion that he was getting more "free" time than I, somehow sneaking an individual life into the equation of our family one, where I had failed to do so…and of course the blame for that failure, which I had unfairly placed on him. Was there something else there? Beneath it all?

"Yes," I said finally, "I'll try. Thanks, Dad." He seemed satisfied with this, smiled and turned his attention to the dessert menu.

The possibility that there was something there between me and Zach kept me from walking away and had for many moons. That and the exhausting consideration of how to co-parent from two different homes, or even towns. My dad and I finished our desserts without talking, but even the small foray we had taken into communication had shifted our relationship toward one another, so that I felt warmer somehow. I felt aware of a new kind of communion where mingled not only our shared history but our shared present, wherein we could talk frankly, if metaphorically, about our lives.

Tomorrow we would escort my grandfather's casket onto an airplane. We would be guided onto the tarmac to observe its loading into the cargo hold of a commercial jet. The people in the airport would watch solemnly from the vast windows, each of them imagining our story and responding to us accordingly, but they would be far from us. My father and I would be moving inside a bubble, accompanied by Officer Houseman, the membrane between us melting, so that we seemed to share a body, as we shared this history, this hurt.

Chapter Twelve

December 1998, Conway, Arkansas

When we arrived at the funeral home in Conway, the casket was opened and, miraculously, the violets I had laid inside it, where Grandpa Charlie's heart would have been, were pristine, unwilted and unbruised by the passage of two days' time inside the closed coffin. I would consider it a small miracle and a sign, though I had received no such sign from Grandma Esther. No affirmation of the connection between her and my grandfather. Grandpa Charlie would finally be laid to rest this week among the graves of family, beneath the waves of sadness and relief that would move among those still living, as they covered what remained of his mortal shell with Arkansas dirt.

That night I called Zach in San Diego. The weather was unusually warm, he said, and earlier that day he had let Zee play in the sand on the beach in a T-shirt and jeans, barefooted and bareheaded. I could picture him on his mother's deck overlooking the sea now, his feet up on the banister, a longneck bottle in his hand. He would be winding down with the sunset and a little Bob Dylan. He would be quietly wondering what was happening in my heart, in my head.

The contrast between that image, suffused with Zach's tranquility, and the scene I inhabited at the moment was extreme. I was holding the receiver of the phone to my ear with my shoulder while struggling to make the small space heater in my room work. We were staying with Uncle Eddie and his wife Maxine in their little farmhouse. The rooms we were assigned were rarely used, and Uncle Eddie had forgotten to open them up to circulate the air and the heat. Aunt Maxine had upbraided him heartily, cataloguing all that she had done to prepare for our visit, matched against the *one thing* she had asked him to do. He had grunted unapologetically and led us up to our floor, the wooden stairs creaking under his weight with each step. Right then, on the phone with Zach, I could see my breath.

"Service is tomorrow," I told him. "This whole trip seems kind of protracted, like we're moving in slow motion, you know?"

"Yeah," he said noncommittally. I thought I could hear the ocean in the background, but no, I decided, it was just his voice. Something stirred in me, softly, softly.

"There's going to be a flyover...F-15's. I guess that's the kind of jet they use now." Zach waited for me to continue. "Missing man formation. That's when one of the planes flies straight up and disappears into the clouds or whatever."

"Yeah, I know." He spoke softly, sweetly.

"My dad has been asked to receive the flag. You know how they do that at the end of a military burial?"

"Mm-hmm," he said.

"It's a big deal. It means a lot to him. My mom and my brother fly in tomorrow morning early. Robby had his last exam today."

"How is your mom?" he asked, knowing that she had just had her five-years-out oncologist appointment.

"She's good," I said. "Clean bill of health!"

"Awesome," he said, and I could hear that he was genuinely relieved. And then, "How are *you* doing, Meg?"

"I'm good," I said, and after a moment again, "Yeah, good."

"Good."

"Zach, I feel kind of numb right now." He knew what I meant, because the question's completion hovered somewhere in the lines that connected us by telephone. *How are you doing with us?* he wanted to know. I was ashamed of what I said, but he deserved the truth. Again, he waited for me to continue. "I don't know what to do. I don't want to give up, but…"

"Then don't." It was simple for Zach. "Don't." Here was a man who had abandoned his surf-chasing life to be near me and our daughter. Who had accepted a job at a magazine he only vaguely respected in order to provide us with stability. To make us look like a family and ultimately feel like one. A small amount of bitterness had crept in, in the past two years that I had shut him out, but he seemed to put that away from him now. "I'll court you, Meg. I'll *make* you remember. Let me do that."

I felt weary and a little sick to my stomach, but vaguely grateful. He was willing to hold on for the both of us, I could see. Where I was ready to let go my hold of the boat's railing, sink to the bottom of the sea of my self-imposed isolation, Zach had a firm grip on my wrists and was straining to keep us both on board. I was still struggling to integrate Zee into this elaborate metaphor in my head when he spoke again.

"Remember that day you told me about? The one right after I met you? When you went down to Hazards and walked into the water fully clothed?"

"Yeah, of course I do," I said. The sharing of that memory had marked an intimate moment in our early friendship. The new trust that was just taking shape. I had told Zach about how I had felt that day, lifted out of my body but alive and awake and new somehow. I had told him of the glistening wetsuits lined up like seals along the rocks. Of the boys in the water, naked and wild with light. Hooting and laughing over and inside of the curling waves that day. I had told him, too, about the thing that broke loose in me that day. How the experience of floating there beneath an enormous sun in a clear blue sky, listening to the effervescent music of the moving water around my ears, had felt like a sacred ablution. A defining moment somehow, though itself undefinable.

"I was there," he said.

"What?"

"I was there. The boy who was doing all the hollering." He waited for me to speak but sensing the catch in my throat I did not. "It was me."

"Why didn't you tell me?"

"I don't know. At the time I hadn't recognized you. You were so far away, on the inside, and I had only met you the once. You were a silhouette. A backlit stranger. An angel. But then when you told me about it later. About how it had been the day after I met you—I knew right away. But it seemed so sacred to you. Your solitude seemed inviolate. And important," he said. "I thought that should be preserved."

It had been important. He was right. It would have changed things to know that he had been there, had seen me and, most likely, found me strange. But now. To know that he was there all the time. When I was so sure I had been alone.

"I love you, Meg. I love you so much." It broke something inside to hear the words. I was deep in thought, enveloped in the way my sense of us was reconfiguring itself, almost like a repagination, or a Jacob's ladder. This new sense of an old memory picked up like the next block in the wooden toy, colorful ribbons spilling over one another as all the pieces adjusted to their new arrangement, their new fulcrum, as it were: me in that transformative moment, but with Zach inside of it, just along the periphery, vulnerable in his nakedness but free. *So free.* It spoke of the freedom that was mine to have. It always had. But now, just now, the ocean took on Zach's voice. Had it not always been his voice? Reminding me how to love?

My conviction about my feelings just then could not match his, and I was still reeling from the thoughts swirling in my head, so I remained silent.

"Will you let me try?" he said. To court me? To woo me again? It was not so great a request. It asked of me inaction. I had the energy for that. Wasn't that what I had been doing for the past year or more? *Not* acting?

"Yes. We can try," I said. I heard a low sigh and then a gathering of breath on the other end of the phone. I could feel his determination in his breathing, in the moment it took for him to say all that he had to say.

"Thank you. Thank you, Meg." And again, "I love you."

"Thank *you*, Zach. You are so strong. So sure of everything." He might have said back to me, *Is it so difficult to be sure? Is it so much to ask to define what I am to you?* But he did not.

"Good night, Meghann Faye."

"Good night, Zach. Kiss that baby girl for me."

"I will. Night night."

At the service the next day, Violet would be absent from the company, and no one would mention her there. Had I believed that she would come, I would have insisted upon the invitation being extended, but she had not left her house in years and she had failed to raise even an eyebrow in the face of the news. Perhaps in her heart she had buried Charlie Carroll long ago, when they had set the empty coffin in the ground. Perhaps like my father, she had allowed the chapter to be closed with the fact of his absence from her life. She had lost her husband when she was thirty and her boys were only babes. That was all. *That was all.*

The ceremony in the church was beautiful, simple, and I felt very small beneath a vast, vaulted ceiling and the colored light of slanting stained glass. There was a discreet media crew who were there to cover such an unlikely event as the forty-four-years-late burial of an American soldier. He had been brought home at last through the tenacious efforts of a devoted team of researchers and scientists and as the result of a first-time collaboration among the Chinese, Russian and American governments since well before the Cold War began. The story merited a five-minute spot on CNN, it turned out, and later a profile in a NOVA documentary.

I sat next to my father and wept, well aware of the incomprehensibility of my tears to those around me but unable to stop them from coming. The bizarre combination of sadness and relief I felt for my father, and the growing awareness of just how deeply related we are to those who have begotten us, whether we knew them or not, overwhelmed my senses and burned my eyes.

On a large cherry wood easel next to the casket stood a framed image. My Uncle Lawrence had commissioned a painting of my grandfather. It was done from a photograph that had been taken of him kneeling next to his F-86. His long hands rested at his knee, one holding the wrist of the other. In his eyes, a softness, a depth and yes, a little mischief. Next to him on the fuselage was a large painted purple flower and the word, in a curvaceous scrawl: *Violet.* He looked just like my dad. Especially in photos from when my dad was in his thirties, in my own memories of that time period, when I was eleven, twelve, thirteen years old. With that image looming above the absent corpus of the man, here in the First United Methodist Church of Conway, I felt I understood why Violet found it so difficult to be in a room with my father. To listen to his voice, no doubt also redolent of Charlie's, to see his face, the chiseled replica of the man she had loved.

I knew, even as these thoughts filled my mind, that so much of what I attributed to Violet was a projection. I had never allowed, as my great uncles had, for the thought that she was just heartless. Inherently incapable of loving, incapable of knowing how to care for another. In my imaginings, she was simply broken, irreparably. My father and his brothers, all their half-siblings who followed, and certainly the men who had loved Violet in Charlie Carroll's wake, were victims of the same loss. How a single death, a single puncture in the blue sky of a life, can reach so many people, like ripples on water, expanding endlessly. How they can reach across generations and across families, so that one grief is indistinguishable from another.

And now, my own grief, unique too in its qualities. Mine was nameless now. It had grown to encompass so many things, including my own inability to open myself fully to Zach, receive his love. It infused my own love for my daughter, so that I could not extricate my love from my fear, and when I kissed Zee goodbye, whether for an hour or a day, the awareness was always there that it could easily be the last time I experienced that pleasure. I knew that my experiences had given me a rare glimpse into the negative image of *having*, so that I might with grace appreciate what was mine. But had it not also marred my confidence to move in my life, free of terror's grip on my shoulder? Had it not also weighted my love with fear, crushing in its heaviness?

When I passed the casket in the procession of family along the front of the congregation and down the aisle to exit, I leaned over my grandfather's Air Force uniform in its silken bed. It was decorated with myriad pins and medals representing his valor, his integrity, his sacrifice. Beneath that coat, I knew, lay the rubble of a body that had been able, strong, and had engendered my father and thus my own family line. I lifted the violets to my lips and kissed them, again silently acknowledging my grandmother for whom I felt I held sacred space, even though she would never acknowledge the act or me as her son's daughter.

In my mind's eye, I saw her at home in Turlock, her eyes closed behind the lenses of her glasses and the moving reflection of a soundless sitcom rerun. She was singing the Patti Page song I knew her to have sung when my father was Matty. Matty in his cowboy boots, Matty with a dollop of Tres Flores pomade in his golden brown tuft of hair, Matty the middle son of a fledgling marriage. Matty the boy who could make her smile with his love of stories, his insatiable curiosity about the world, his tentative touch. Matty who had, like the others, been absorbed into her grief and the unmemory that haunted her for a lifetime.

"Another time, another place, we'll be together again." Her voice was sultry, textured by years of smoking cigarettes, but it was lovely, just as my father had described it, his admiration spilling like rings of light from his lips, a disturbance in the water. Her voice grew in strength as I listened: "This kiss, this same embrace, will be more wonderful then. Though goodbye is a sad time, be glad we had time to fall in love. I leave my love with you…

"When shadows grow, I miss the glow that only you can provide. But then, I'll just pretend you're still right here at my side. Now give me once more that kiss I adore, then I'll let you go, but we'll meet another time, another place, I know."

My mother's hand on my back reminded me of where I was, and I opened my eyes, moved away from the casket and the seeming wormhole that had taken me into my grandmother's living room nearly two thousand miles away. We were ushered down the aisle of the church, out through the foyer and down the walkway into black limousines that brought us out to the cemetery. There spanned for miles, it seemed, headstones pale against rolling green hills swollen with the past weeks' rain, and we walked, following the horse-drawn carriage that bore my grandfather's coffin, draped over with the American flag. The day was overcast, which only intensified the gold sun as it broke through clouds heavy with their burden but holding off, holding off.

There was a twenty-one-gun salute by young cadets in a stoic line, each of whom must have been aware even then of the fine line between their own realities and the one represented here. How many of them would be shipped out in time to the former Yugoslavia or, in five years Afghanistan, and run the risk of never returning, perhaps disappearing into the oblivion of MIA and KIA and the accompanying heroism of those abbreviated conditions.

Then the F-15's in their missing man formation, and the silence of people taken up into the rumbling noise of jet engines as a lone aircraft lifted itself up and away from its cohorts, flew straight up into clouds fretted with sunlight, until we could no longer see it.

It was a day that spilled away from us, opening out onto our shared past, our shared future. The common thread of our DNA and the stories of our loving, our losing, our healing and our denial, spanned the distance and disappeared in either direction. "Pre-history" in one direction and in the other, a future too far out to envision but present and panting its impending life. I longed for Zee, and though I had stopped nursing her over a year before, I felt that longing in my breasts, the sensation of milk dropping in to ducts that were long since dry. *How a mother never stops nurturing, even with the body,* I thought, and as always it brought me back to the anomaly of Grandma Esther, her cold distance from us all. My thoughts returned to Zach, too, I had to admit. To the comfort his presence here might have provided, had I invited it.

That night I had another dream. In this one I inhabited the painting of my grandfather and his F-86 Sabre Jet. I touched the lettering that comprised my grandmother's name, let my forehead fall to touch the violet petals painted there. My grandfather was frozen in his position next to the plane and could not see me or hear my soft breathing nearby. I dared not touch him but instead moved around him, observing him, the patriarch of my family: the young man who never grew old and was now, in this moment, barely my senior. In the wings, for we occupied a stage of sorts, I could hear my grandmother's voice, her haunting song, and I called to her, but she too seemed unable to hear me. The image of my grandfather seemed to lose substance under the spell of the incantation, so that it vibrated, matching the notes that Violet uttered. I shook my head, beginning to understand what was happening, but I was powerless to stop it. Grandpa Charlie's image seemed to disintegrate and turn to particles and finally ash. The residue slowly lifted on the air and disappeared in the space between my body and the darkness that bound the dream. When it was gone, so was Violet's voice, and I was left alone.

I saw then that the plane was gone, too, and that I occupied the center position on a large stage. In the audience were all of my family members: my mother and father, holding hands. My brother. Zach and Azizah. And there was a sea of other bodies whose faces I could not bring into focus but whom I knew were related to me. They all watched me, silent and rapt. Just as I opened my mouth to speak, there was a jarring alarm that rang into the space relentlessly and which, finally, drew me out of the dream and into the small space in Uncle Eddie's upstairs guest room. Buried beneath handmade quilts and an electric blanket I was sure was radiating me but which I could not relinquish because of the cold, I opened my eyes and knew where I was. I knew where I was and I knew the lines that were mine to speak.

Chapter Thirteen

March 1999, San Luis Obispo, California

When Zach and Zee picked me up at the airport, her little legs could not carry her fast enough toward me, and she nearly tumbled as she ran in the direction of the gate. It was so good to have her in my arms again, and I buried my face in her curly black hair, kissed her chubby little neck, making her fall into a fit of giggles and squirm in my embrace. It was good to see Zach, too, and he allowed my greeting to be a full body hug and not a kiss. It was the touch I needed, the touch I could give. He took my carry-on and my hand, and together we walked to the baggage claim, Zee chattering happily on my hip, my right arm encircling her and holding her body close to me.

This was the family I was growing, whether I had planned it or not. It was the nucleus that had become the gravitational center of my world. I would learn to be who I was inside of it: a poet, a woman, an athlete, and also a mother and partner. I would learn that one role did not diminish another and that giving myself to Zach did not mean relinquishing my self but rather sharing it. It was a generous act, sharing one's life with another, and I found that I was capable of it. I wondered how many young partnerships disintegrated because of impatience, because of disbelief in their own origins and the amnesia of early childrearing. I knew myself as lucky, too, to have had Zach and his infinite patience, his infinite faith, to compensate for my own shortfall in both of those areas.

I thanked the heavens that he had not let go, too, had not let me sink into the ocean of my isolation, though I had as much as begged him to do so. Perhaps it is always that way in the relationships that survive, that when one partner is weak, the other finds strength, and vice versa. Whatever it was, whether infinite luck on my part or the abiding course of a love patterned in the stars, I was grateful. Full of gratitude and for once, *not grasping.*

On March second, 1999, two months after we laid Grandpa Charlie in the ground almost to the day, Violet closed her eyes for the last time. Without having given any indication that she knew or cared about the momentous events around the recovery of his body and his aircraft, without any sign of distress at all, she lay down on her bed beneath a chenille bedspread and went to sleep. Her neighbor Hedda James found her the next day when she stopped by to deliver a quart of milk and half a dozen eggs from the farmers' market. The front door was unlatched, and the house was still dark and quiet from the night before. Mrs. James had put the items in the refrigerator and braved the cavernous hallway to the back bedroom.

"Esther?" she had called. "Esther, you here?" The floorboards had creaked beneath her steps, and she had paused at the door, heard it groan as it swung slowly open against the light pressure of her hand. Violet looked like she was sleeping, but Mrs. James knew right away by the gray cast of her cheeks, the stillness of her chest, that she was gone. She looked tiny beneath the white cover embellished with lavender flowers. Her hair was contained in a fine little ponytail tied neatly with a thick length of pink crafting yarn. Her glasses were folded and tidily stowed on the bedside table, her slippers lined up just so, where she had left them and climbed into her bier. Her hands were folded over her ribs, as if she had arranged herself for her departure.

"Good night," she had said into the stale air of the old farmhouse. The house that had held all of her secrets and whispered them back to her in the years she had lived there alone, letting the stories steep like tea in the fluid of her life from day to day. Without judgment. Without shame. They were what they were, and she was what she was. She had lived one way and not another. She had survived the best that she could. And she had loved. She had loved deeply and privately, and her love, perhaps because she had been so consumed by it, because she had not known how to release herself from it, had broken her.

Attachment is a powerful thing. According to Buddhist philosophy, I had learned, that kind of desire is the root of all suffering. Violet had let her desire crush her under its weight, so that it had left her incapable of carrying any other love or thought. What remained in the wake of a disintegrated self: fear. And Violet let it swallow her whole. Somewhere along the periphery of this understanding of her, there was the awareness of the role my imagination played in fleshing it out. My own desire gave Violet's story its details, adorned her with the kind of love I wanted her to have. But I had let the story grow, because I needed to.

When the dust had settled, and Violet had failed to nourish any life but the one barely sustained by her own anemic heart, she had found herself alone. This is how she had spent the last twenty-six years of her life. She had spent her private life grasping; her public life, such as it was, had been spent hiding. Sleep walking through her interactions with others, so as to keep the fear, like a threatening animal, a wild thing, at bay. Those years were punctuated, of course, by obligatory visits from her two remaining sons and from Hedda James, whose happy generosity kept her stocked with life's necessities and the occasional conversation. The later years were marked, too, by intrepid little advances by her granddaughter whose desire mirrored her own and frightened Violet even more.

That is what I was to her, I think. I held a mirror up to her, as she did for me, and our dissimilarities were as disconcerting as our likenesses. My insistence on knowing--*something, anything*--about what we were, what our shared history was…it was more than she could bear. I asked too much, continually. Believed, in my naiveté, that my perfect intention transcended all. That my innocence had the power to break through to a heart that must still be warm and alive somewhere in the shell she presented as her exterior self. I had been wrong. Sometimes we are. It is no more complex than that: human miscalculation.

What I had not been wrong about was Violet's interior life. In the end I believed that only the kind of attachment I had imagined up for her could have given her the power to will her own passage. I think the desire to die had been haunting her for years, but she needed to *know*, in this life and with utter certainty, that Charlie was gone. She needed to know that he had in fact died that last cold September day, just as she had believed in her heart from the moment that black car had pulled onto her road in Bradford, Arkansas. That moment in which she, standing with Baby on her hip, broom in hand, had felt herself shatter, like so many shards of glass. With that certainty, delivered up nearly forty-five years late but unequivocally nonetheless, she could finally let go. She slipped into the ether with no fanfare. Just hope. Finally, hope.

Chapter Fourteen

March 1999, Turlock, California

Violet's funeral service was bizarre, to say the least. Strange how marriage and death are the two things that have the power to bring a family together, against the odds of lives that are otherwise oriented toward complete distance and separation. My father and his brother Sebastian had not seen each other in years and could not have picked any of their half-siblings out of a line-up, not having seen any of them since their slow removal from their mother's home and life. Violet's death brought every last one of them together. And it brought me, Zach and Azizah, as a unit, to her graveside to witness the motley reunion of others.

Grandma Esther had never once flown in an airplane, and it was decided by my parents that she would not start now. It was decided, too, that she had moved here, to California, had abandoned any attachment to Arkansas and any of its people, least of all my grandfather's brothers, two of whom still lived there and had not spoken her name in nearly half a century. It was decided that Grandma Esther would be buried in Turlock, California, near my mother's family. Close to the home she had not left except to go to the market and twice to visit a doctor in the last twenty-five years.

The drive out to the little cemetery in Turlock was warm, even though it was March, and the sky was clear and big above us. I opened the window and let the early spring air circulate inside the car, my eyes flitting among the rows of trees as we passed orchard after orchard. Zee sang a little song from her car seat behind me. "This little light of mine, I'm gonna' let it shine," she chirped sweetly in her three-and-a-half-year-old garble. "Won't let anyone 'whoo' it out," she sang around a baby tooth smile, blowing her index finger in lieu of a candle. We passed mounds of fertilizer, too, held down by heavy black tarps weighted with old tires, and cows grazing on corn products with their heads between metal bars. Green hills rose beyond them in the distance, a gentle mockery of their artificially circumscribed bovine lives.

Zach put his hand on mine from time to time during the three-hour drive over from my parents' house in Santa Cruz. Quietly present. The "central cedar pole" to my "silken tent." The warm air moved across my face as we rode, and I closed my eyes, breathing in the rich odor of soil, grass and post-rain asphalt. I felt clear-headed and knew that we drove now to a second anachronistic funeral. Grandma Esther, too, had died long before there was a body to bury. She had occupied that body for so many years in a sleep walking state that resembled death more than it did life. And now, she rested.

At the funeral beneath a white tent my father, who inherited his mother's musical ear and angelic voice, played a little karaoke machine and sang "Another Time, Another Place." Our extended family, related by halves, stood under the tent, women lifting their heels out of the soft grass at intervals, men shifting and tugging at their collars. There were the twins, Joe and Edie, with their families. Uncle Joe was oddly fair with his blond mass of hair, but Edie, without knowing it, appeared as a ghost of her mother's past life. There were the Pruitt sisters, Heather and Amelia. Both had jet black hair and puckered pink lips, but Heather's breasts and belly swelled with her third pregnancy while Amelia, the youngest of Violet's children, had remained obstinately single. Though she was my aunt by blood, we were very close in age and could have been cousins instead.

My dad, not having seen either of the girls since their removal from Violet's house that rainy day in 1971, kept scanning them again and again, as if to reconcile something vaguely out of place. Perhaps it was the fact of Heather with her daughter, now the age she had been when he had seen her last and had unfurled her fingers from their hold on the handle of Violet's iron. He had lifted her tenderly from the chair upon which she stood, draped a tiny sweater around her thin shoulders and made the phone call to Aunt Elizabeth. Aunt Elizabeth was present too, now a white-headed lady of nearly seventy but still with erect carriage and the vague disdain of one who considers herself above the company.

My mother had looped her arm inside my father's and would touch his chest from time to time, her palm flat as if to feel his heart. Their union was so apparent here. This was the assembly of all the bits of my father's history, ones he had released into the blue sky of forgetting and ones he had kept, like secret treasures, tucked deep in the recesses of his mind. My mother, having known and loved him since she was a girl of fourteen, provided the counterbalance to the weight of all these people in his sensibility, perhaps most of all because together they had supplanted the tangle of them with their own seeds of love and creation. My mother's dark brown hair was now interspersed with white, but otherwise, she had changed surprisingly little in the twenty-eight years they had been married. My brother stood on my dad's other side, stoic and reserved for the occasion. The mischievous twinkle in the Carroll eyes he bore was the only evidence of the entertainment he derived in observing this menagerie of half-relatives.

Beyond them: my Uncle Seb, also with his grown daughter, Karen. Karen's blue eyes were reminiscent of her mother who, in the throes of her own searching, had left Uncle Seb and their two children to fend for themselves when Karen's brother Max was still a baby. Karen had done her best to raise her little brother, but Max had been in and out of jail since he had come of age. He was there now, while the rest of his family gathered for the funeral of someone he never knew but whose DNA fretted his own and was responsible for his hairline, his angelic singing voice, and his spindly gait which, Karen noticed, appeared in different configurations in these strangers to herself.

The other absence was my Uncle Ricky, long ago buried in Conway, preserved in his brothers' minds as a nineteen-year-old boy at the helm of a helicopter. He would have been the eldest of Violet's sons, would have now been fifty years old and perhaps had children and grandchildren of his own. A shadow limb on the body of this piece-meal family.

The funeral was imbued with quiet awe, as the company curiously observed half-sisters and half-brothers. Here, a familiar jaw-line, there a known voice issuing from the mouth of a virtual stranger. Nothing in common but blood, the odd shared characteristic, and the strange life and death of the woman they lowered into the ground. Esther Violet Carroll. Blake. Pruitt. Strands of self, spanning across a country, drawn back together to acknowledge her departure from a life she had forfeited long ago.

To close the service I was invited to stand behind the spindly black music stand that careened from its place on the uneven grass. I read aloud. I read to Violet.

The Long Goodbye

You have become a myth for me.
Some hint of self, enigmatic reflection
of my history. You take with you
all the secrets we wanted to hear you
speak, all of the reasons we imagined up—
or never could. How do I say goodbye to you?

Something about you that was lovely,
beautiful. Blazing comet moving
in your irregular orbit, leaving sparks, light
in your wake, but never pausing to look back
and see what you had sown.

If the night sky was your arena,
you are still moving there now,
your broken heart finally shed and left
on some suburban lawn where it fell
as your soul lifted on air and became light,
weightless for the first time in so many years.

O, we languish in the light that trails behind you,
lift our faces and make our goodbye
the kind of greeting we wanted you to have.
Welcome to the sky, welcome to freedom,
welcome to the liberation of existing
in memory alone. Glide into what you always
wanted to be. I don't presume. I know.
Because it's what we all want.

Anonymity somehow. The kind of freedom
that means not shrinking from the truth.

Blessings upon you, Violet. You were brave
and this life was again and again unkind,
each year a moment in a very long goodbye.

Because none of us lived in Turlock, my mother had decided to rent a suite at a large ranch-style hotel there, so that the family would have a place to gather after the graveside service. Though neither of my parents was a big drinker, because of their nervousness over being the default hosts of this unlikely gathering of blood-related strangers, she made sure there was plenty of wine and beer on hand in coolers, as well as several catered trays of finger foods to fend off afternoon hunger and provide the niceties of such an occasion.

People made their way to the hotel suite slowly, trickling in through the enclosed atrium onto which two levels of rooms opened. It was close and hot in the room at first, so the earlier guests stood around sweating and making small talk. My brother, still a college student then, farmed out beers immediately, well aware of the need to blur the focus, soften the edges of this outlandish scene. My father moved as if in slow motion, talking in his low, gravelly voice to now a half-sister, now a half-brother, engaging warily in the unwieldy task of closing the abysmal gap of time looming among them all. He must have known there was no way to catch them up to speed with what had grown into his life after they had been lifted out of it, one by one. And *how,* how to attend to learning the vast expanse of life that had also bloomed on their side of that gulf?

"Meggie?" I heard the diminutive version of my name spoken by a voice that sounded a lot like Grandma Esther's, and when I turned to face her was mildly shocked to see her face, as well. But of course it was not Violet, who had lived well beyond the age of the woman who addressed me now. It was my "Aunt" Edie, I had learned during the service, one of the twins Violet had had with Dennis Blake. She had Violet's eyes, her long black hair shot through with gray, and she had Violet's pointed chin; but here, in these eyes, was a softness I had never seen in my grandmother's face.

"I'm your Aunt Edie," she said, extending her hand awkwardly, and then drawing me to her in a gentle embrace. I could feel her kindness, her genuineness just in her touch. She smelled of jasmine, and that too reminded me of Violet. She seemed a walking contradiction.

"Yes, hi, I— Nice to meet you," I said. *I've heard so much about you?* No. *Great to finally meet you?* No. *You look exactly like your mother, it's freaky?* No.

"Your daddy's song was beautiful," she said, tipping her head in his direction. She wore a wool pencil skirt and a matching jacket, a little outdated and a little too warm for the weather, but proper, tidy. Her flesh colored pantyhose made tiny creases at her ankles, and her fingernails were clipped close, clean.

"Yeah, he got Grandma Esther's voice. He says she used to sing that song."

"Yeah, he told me that. I don't have very many memories of her. I remember your daddy, though. He used to read books to me when I was a little girl. He's a good man, your daddy."

It was true, and I nodded my assent. How had he broken the cycle of poverty and, harder to do, I think, lovelessness? In his older brother, it had turned to bile in his gut, had driven him to the sky, to war and a personal recklessness that may have been as much to blame for his death as enemy fire. In his younger brother it had turned to a kind of phlegmatic hopelessness that had drained a marriage and his firstborn son, sent his wife into infidelity and his boy to petty crime and a series of jail sentences. But my dad. He had changed the way things were. Things were one way, and he had changed them. For himself and his progeny. It was no small feat.

"You know, you look a lot like my mama." It was a simple observation, and Aunt Edie's eyes roamed over my forehead, my hair, my nose and mouth. "A lot like her," she said rather breathlessly. It occurred to me that when little Edie had been taken away from her, Violet would have been probably somewhere between us in age. I must have looked, to Edie's eye, like a ghost. I wondered if my voice sounded like hers, too, though as I was tone deaf, I had no illusions about having inherited her singing talent. We stood there awkwardly, two ghosts taking each other in, tentative to speak or move.

Beyond Aunt Edie, I could see my brother talking surreptitiously with Uncle Joe, her twin brother, who was known to suffer from rheumatoid arthritis and had a prescription for medical marijuana. Uncle Joe was fishing in his pocket for the keys to his new-to-him Camaro, and I could see them conspiring together. Strange how smokers will find each other in a crowd, for they had been strangers to one another until this moment. Now, at the funeral of our grandmother, they were instant comrades. My brother giggled ironically and winked at me as they passed me on their way to the door.

The tension in the crowd, I noticed, had begun to decline, the beer and wine flowing generously now. With the dearth of shared stories to be told, singular ones were being sung into the air. Names unfamiliar to the listeners and details foreign, the stories bridged the gap that had been so apparent in the beginning. The alcohol had generated a sense of connection that was only partly imagined, for indeed the blood that moved in their veins, a little more freely now, carried the genetic codes that had produced all of them and was responsible for their vague resemblance to one another.

"I enjoyed your poem," Aunt Edie said. "It was real nice, Meggie."

"Thank you."

"You know, I think she just withered after Charlie died. Everything that came after, us— Well, I don't think she really had it in her." It was the first time anyone had supported my romantic view of Violet. The first time anyone had breathed a word of such faith in the love between my grandmother and grandfather. I searched for more in her eyes, but I found only compassion there, a little wistfulness. She meant what she said. And that was all I needed.

"Thank you, Aunt Edie," I said to her. With my hands in hers, Aunt Edie kissed me on the cheek, gazed once more warmly into my face, and was absorbed by the strange congregation of our relatives. Needing a reprieve, wanting just a moment's rest, I opened the door of the suite and stepped out onto the landing overlooking the atrium.

Zach and Zee had been doing laps around the courtyard, had stopped to watch two children splashing in the swimming pool at its center. The children, a sister and a brother perhaps, were climbing over one another and a colorful blow-up raft with a horse's head. I leaned my forearms on the banister and watched as Zach and Zee knelt beneath the tall trees rising from planters cut in the concrete. They were looking at something small, a displaced caterpillar or a ladybug perhaps. Zee wore polka dotted leggings and a knit cotton dress my mother had bought her; her curls were somewhat managed by a matching headband. Even from this distance I could see her dimples.

Zach glanced up and saw me, pointed up to show Zee that I was there. Her eyes became wide, and she waved and started calling loudly, wanting to share with me what they were doing there, what they had seen. I laughed and shook my head, pressing my index finger to my lips. Zach laughed, too, and hushed her, drawing her head to his shoulder and giving her a squeeze, probably explaining how she could not call her whole story across the atrium and up a floor but would have to wait until we came together again.

I was thinking about this when my brother sidled by me, his eyes small and red, a huge grin on his smooth face. Uncle Joe followed behind, equally stony and behaving like a guilty schoolboy. Incredulously, I followed them back inside to find that the assembly had fallen into a further declension, though everyone seemed to be having a good time. It felt like a keg party now, and with the alcohol nearly gone, my brother had talked my parents and Uncle Seb into making a makeshift pipe by coring an apple from Zee's snack bag and smoking out in the bathroom.

All this was still going on when Zach and Zee came back to the suite. I met them at the door and kissed them both good night, Zach grinning as he caught glimpses over my shoulder of the circus-like atmosphere that had developed in the room. At the moment, Amelia appeared to be demonstrating a cheerleading move before a captive audience. I pulled the door nearly closed.

"Night night, Mommy," said Zee, kissing me three times. Once on each eye and once on my lips, our goodnight ritual. I returned the kisses and kissed Zach, too. With my family spiraling into the incongruity of their meeting behind me, laughter rising above the din of their shared disappointments, their hauntingly similar griefs, Zach put his hand on the small of my back and pressed the kiss. A little more insistently. A little more firmly. When he released me I saw determination in his face. Zee giggled now at the level of our knees, where some great half uncle or other had poked his head out the door and was making silly faces at her. Someone inside had begun to sing an Elvis Presley song.

Zach and I met eyes again and could not resist the laughter that rose in our own hearts. "It's funny, right?" I said to him, as if seeking his approval. He grinned and nodded.

"Yeah. It's funny." And we both broke out into a trill of laughter again. It *was* funny. Bizarre and painful, filled with strangeness and hilarity. It was my family, my history, here in the middle of Nowhere, California. Desert heat in March, drunken assembly of mourners howling their dissonance into the atrium of the San Phillipe Inn, soothing their broken loves with song, with story. And it was *my* story, as I had written it, as it had grown in me and culminated here.

Violet would be pleased, I thought. It was a fitting menagerie of defunct mourners that had gathered to mark her passage. What she had failed to knit together with love fell together now, for a single night, like atoms falling from the sky. Landing as they might. Landing outrageously, lightly, beautifully, as they might.

Zach pressed my hand and kissed me again, letting his lips linger against mine, before leading Zee down the hall to our room. I watched them go, considering what had just passed between us. It was the fist time in a long time that I had not demurred when Zach kissed me. And also, there was the fact of his assertiveness. How he had given the kiss but also, he had taken it. It spoke of a knowing that, somewhere between the last time we had kissed and now, he had grown sure of. There was the distant recollection that stirred in my ribcage…of longing satisfied. Of eros refining itself through touch. It felt good. It felt a lot like clarity, if fleeting, and I decided to remember that feeling. Bring it to the fore, rather than press it from me, as I knew I had done before.

The night began to wind down after that, and it culminated, after my dad's stint with his head in the hotel toilet bowl, and after Amelia had changed into some dry clothes, at a long table in the hotel restaurant. Just when I had thought things could not get any wilder, Amelia had taken a fully clothed lap swim on a dare. She had come up laughing hysterically between sobs and mascara-blackened tears only somewhat disguised by the chlorine water dripping from her hair. Now we all sat at a table punctuated by ridiculously ornate candelabras and laden with a veritable feast of roast chicken and heirloom potatoes.

It was only eight o'clock after all, and everyone was starving. The dinner was served family style, and I sat next to my Aunt Amelia, only two years my senior, who fretted the entire time, paranoid over Aunt Elizabeth's judgment of her inappropriate behavior.

"Meg, what will my Aunt Elizabeth think?" she whined "At my own mother's funeral? And with a white shirt on!" She had scrambled from the pool, and her sister and I had herded her into her hotel room so quickly that hardly anyone had seen. I laughed at her paranoia and tried to calm her down with reassuring platitudes and by getting her to eat. The pressure of such a wholly inconceivable life event had pushed her around, made her behave in such an uncharacteristic way. She had prayed to her God before the service had begun to imbue her with confidence and a sense of self-preservation. Her prayer had been answered, it seemed, by a God with a sense of humor.

Perhaps it was also the knowledge that we would never come together like this again that impelled us to behave so rashly, so urgently. *Why would we?* Perhaps when one of us died. Or got married. But probably not. It could only have been our fear and our love that governed this bizarre parade of genetically inspired shenanigans. Was there anything else?

I remember having sunk into bed that night with Zach, Zee wedged insistently between us in the warm little pod of our linked bodies. The sensation of silence and stillness after the scene in the San Phillipe dining room had been a relief. Everyone had managed to tumble to their rooms or to their cars, sobered by the food and by having been seated facing one another under the yellow lights of the restaurant. I had pushed my feet between Zach's calves and found his forehead with my own. I felt content, and I felt solid, though there was still the gentle lilt of intoxication that rocked me in my near sleep. I felt that in the midst of all this chaos, I had somehow found my way home. It was the place that had always been home to me: Zach's heart and the experience of life that we shared. At the center of all of this: our daughter, "the powerful, the strong."

Night had fallen on the story of Violet's life. The one I had grown in my heart since I was a teenager. In the wake of her existence, it all seemed perfectly true, what I had heard and what I had invented. All the story's aspects swam together in my memory until it no longer mattered which had been engendered by recollection and which by invention. It was, all of it combined, the truth. And I was the granddaughter of Esther Violet Carroll. Not an extension of her. Not a mirror of her life or thought. Just the next in a line of Carroll women who could, if they wanted, change things as they were, the way my father had done. The way my grandfather Charlie Carroll had also done in his way.

About the Author

Kim Cope Tait's written works have appeared in literary journals and magazines in the U.S. and abroad. She earned her MFA in Writing: Poetry in 2001 at Vermont College of Fine Arts. Kim is the author of *Element*, a chapbook of poems, and her first novel *Inertia* was published in 2011. She is also the author and voice of the album *Lotus Wheel: Guided Meditations for Relaxation and Healing.* Kim has been practicing yoga and meditation for fifteen years and teaching them for thirteen. Her Lotus Wheel retreats invite yogis and writers of all levels to explore their creativity through yoga asana and the written word.

www.kimcopetait.com

About the Artist

Susan Teare is a free-lance photographer working and living in Vermont and Colorado. Her work has appeared in many books and publications, including *Better Homes and Gardens, This Old House, Organic Gardening* and the highly acclaimed salvage-for-design books, *Salvage Secrets.*

www.susanteare.com

www.ingramcontent.com/pod-product-compliance
Ingram Content Group UK Ltd.
Pitfield, Milton Keynes, MK11 3LW, UK
UKHW041826200726
13854UKWH00002BA/607